FACELESS

FACELESS

THE MYSTERY OF THE CARVED ARROW

ASHWIN KARTHIK

Srishti
PUBLISHERS & DISTRIBUTORS

Srishti Publishers & Distributors
A unit of AJR Publishing LLP
212A, Peacock Lane
Shahpur Jat, New Delhi – 110 049
editorial@srishtipublishers.com

First published by
Srishti Publishers & Distributors in 2021

10 9 8 7 6 5 4 3 2 1

Acknowledgement

I WOULD LIKE TO EXPRESS MY HEARTFELT GRATITUDE TO THOSE WHO helped me stay motivated through the journey of writing this book.

My family, especially my mom, for being the corner-stone of my life and supporting me in all my endeavours.

My friends Mahesh Reddy, Guru Prasad, Ram Kishan Singh Rajput and Ashish Shetty for constantly sharing their comments on the story and helping me make it better.

THE CONVENTION CENTRE IN THE HEART OF THE IT HUB WAS FULL OF A thousand-people-strong audience, holding their breath in anticipation. The atmosphere was charged with excitement, expectations were sky high for the inspired version of world's most popular idea sharing platform, the TEDx talk! The audience was overwhelmingly captivated by the eight speakers on stage, who had shared their thoughts and ideas on a wide variety of topics. That included art, literature, technology, innovation, diversity and inclusion, world economy, entrepreneurship, even sex.

The hall echoed with grand applause for almost every speaker. As people waited for the ninth and last speaker, Anvesha Roy walked in. Elegantly dressed in a saree, a pleasing smile, gleaming eyes full of life and a personality that would force anyone to turn around and look at her again. A female historian, rare in the profession, folded her hands in a *namaste* to the audience. Looking at her, most listeners expected her to talk about something similar to what previous speakers already had. But they were in for a real surprise.

"Propaganda! The technique of making the masses believe what you want them to believe. *Illuminati!* Priory of Sion,

Knights Templar, Da Vinci Code… do they ring some bells in your head? I am sure they do. It is the sweet smell of mystery that lures us, that makes us curious, isn't it? But why is it that every time there is a discussion about secret societies, we think of the western world? What if there *is* an Indian secret society that has remained out of sight since time immemorial?

"This definitely raises questions on the very existence of these unknown nine men. But first let us understand if there was even a possibility of such an organization being formed in the first place. India is a huge land mass, more so when Pakistan and Bangladesh were included. Obviously in such a huge land area, tens of hundreds of small kingdoms popped up. Every king wanted to expand his kingdom and to quench the thirst of ambition, all of them waged wars against each other. Much like today's corporate world or even countries to establish their supremacy in the world order by gaining and winning the trade war.

"The difference between the ancient wars in the battlefield and the modern-day trade wars is that they don't take place in an open battlefield, but from air-conditioned offices. Nonetheless, these wars weakened all the kingdoms. Chandragupta Maurya, along with his teacher, the legendry Chanakya sensed it and thus made up his mind to unify India.

"Both Chanakya and Chandragupta wanted India to be united and strong, so that we could fight away foreign forces that tried to invade us. Their efforts were continued by Ashoka, and the famous battle of Kalinga was a result of these efforts. As the world knows, this war was the cause of death of a hundred thousand people. This also brought in him a life-altering change of embracing peace and giving up violence in every possible way.

"He realized that the best way to rule over people was not by winning over their land or property, but by winning over their hearts! Hence his conversion to Buddhism. He made it the mission of his life to spread peace across borders. He also was aware that knowledge does not always mean wisdom. That is why he called in the nine smartest men of his huge empire and instructed them to build a knowledge base on nine different subjects.

"The nine men were instructed to keep the knowledge base they create, which probably could be a book, very illusive. This was to avoid the knowledge being misused. Probably Ashoka was reluctant to allow the nine geniuses to make the knowledge they gather public due to fear of people with far lesser maturity getting manipulated. Great knowledge, when used for the betterment of humanity could prove as an extraordinary tool. But if it reaches the wrong hands, that want to use it to meet selfish ends, it becomes a deadly weapon! And that would turn disastrous for the existence of life in its entirety.

"This was the very reason, historians believe, that these nine loyal people devised an efficient plan to keep their clan alive through centuries, while they maintained its secrecy. The plan was that each of the nine special people would carry out the tasks assigned to them religiously. But if due to any circumstances they had to opt out of their secret role, they would have to delegate their responsibilities to someone most trustworthy. Someone who would play the role at least equally well, if not better.

"Well, now you might ask me if these nine geniuses existed and indeed were working on something really important. What were they working on? Obviously, the knowledge they attempted to build was in fields that must remain relevant for a long time, despite generations. That is why it could be a double-edged sword! Researchers believe the nine men and their successors gathered vast amount of knowledge in these nine subjects:

- Physiology
- Microbiology
- Alchemy
- Communication
- Gravity
- Cosmogony
- Light
- Sociology
- Propaganda

"Actually, the fact that we have all but forgotten about the existence of such a secret society is the success of these extraordinary people. This indeed in a way is the true success of the secret clan. We do not know much about these people majorly because they did not want us to know about them.

"Not many of us know of the oldest secret societies that could have existed for more than two thousand years. Like many of us believe that great revolutionary minds of the West were an active part of secret societies like the "Freemasons", "Priory of Sion," etc., Indians like Shushruta (who authentically was the first surgeon the world saw), greatest scholars, thinkers, poets like Tenali Ramakrishna and Kalidasa could have been a part of the clan. Modern scientists like Vikram Sarabhai and J.C. Bose are believed to be active participants of such a secret society according to popular conspiracy theories.

"I will conclude by seeding a couple of questions that loom large in my curious mind. If such a secret clan or society was indeed created with a purpose of nationalism and human betterment, are the many conspiracy theories we hear and read about true? Does a secret group of individuals really exist, that staying under the surface controls what happens in and around our lives? How would the state of affairs be, just in case these individuals give up on their oath of non-violence? What if they turn to punish the guilty using the extraordinary knowledge they possess?"

▼

In a nearby five-star hotel, a guest checked-in, introducing himself as Yuyutsu Ghosh, a scientist at the renowned Indian Space Agency. After he settled in his suite, he made a call to the room service and ordered a drink for himself. A few minutes later, a waiter knocked at the door of the suite and sought permission to enter.

From within the suite came a hoarse voice that said, "Come in."

The man entered the suite with a tray over his shoulder on which there was crystal glass that was quarter filled with Glenfiddich whisky. Besides which was a bottle of the same drink.

It was a spacious, bright, and outward facing room, refurbished with teak wood furniture. The guest sat on a huge single sofa opposite the magnificent glass windows offering a view of the hotel pool. The wall opposite to the window had a huge painting of lord Buddha sitting in meditation.

The waiter placed the tray on the table next to his guest and handed over the glass. The guest raised the glass in a toast to the waiter and began to sip his drink as the waiter waited patiently for the guest to make any further requests as he was instructed in his hospitality trainings.

He very patiently stood with folded hands till the guest enjoyed his drink. Yuyutsu asked the attendant to open the bottle. As he was sipping his drink, suddenly his body started having severe convulsions. The convulsions were so bad that the visitor's body literally began bouncing on the large teak sofa.

In his anxiety, he tried holding on to the nearby table, but to no avail. The convulsions resulted in the whisky bottle and the tray smashing into the marble floor. The attendant tried to help, but he did not know how. He tried to hold the man, applying all his might, but could not. He just couldn't hold him.

After the visitor experienced extreme convulsions, his body fell from the sofa to the ground and the man lay unconscious. The alcohol in the glass was spilt, but a few drops stayed in. The attendant was shocked after what he had seen. He fled from the suite at once to the hospitality manager, to tell him that something serious had happened to their famous guest.

The attendant was back to the suite with the officials to see his guest still lying lifeless on the ground. The manager leaned on the guest's chest; he was shell-shocked that he could hardly feel the guest's heartbeat.

"Call 112 and get the ambulance, this man is dying!" He shouted.

The entire hotel staff had queued in the room. In the next ten minutes, the paramedics were in the suite.

The medicos tried all the emergency methods to bring the patient back to consciousness. Even the CPR, but all their efforts were in vain.

The doctors checked the man's pulse one last time and said, "We are sorry, I guess we are late. Your guest is no more, and it looks like a cardiac arrest. We can only give more details after the postmortem. But I advise you call in the local authorities to carry out the formalities."

Losing no time, the hotel management called in the police authorities, who reached the hotel suite soon after.

The hotel was cordoned off; no one could enter or exit from hotel premises until the authorities completed the formalities. Looking at the chaos taking place in the hotel, panic set in amongst the guests staying there. Before anyone could understand what had happened, those who were around saw an arrow flying through the window and getting stuck into the painting on the wall. To the arrowhead was engraved an image.

The image was of a circle with nine spokes and a face of a lion in the center. The arrow created a cloud of doubt over the scientist's death. All the mayhem of the mysterious death trickled to the media in the next couple of hours and became breaking news across news channels.

The city had turned to being on high alert in no time. The news of the death of a scientist and the presence of the engraved arrow spread like wildfire, not just in the city, but across the world. People from all types of media were thronging outside the hotel premises to understand how it all had happened.

Politicians being assassinated is something that has happened across the globe. Even celebrities have been allegedly killed for various reasons. But a scientist's death is clouted with unanswered questions, and raised many eyebrows. The arrow was evidence that this death was much more than just a murder; it was a message. But what was it trying to convey?

As the hotel management along with guests had panicked, one of the hotel staff asked the constable standing in a corner, "Who is the investigating officer for this case? Are we going to be interrogated?"

"Agent Hawk is a master of his own mind! No one can predict what is in his mind. Everyone will be under the scanner till the real culprit is found."

The investigating officer ACP Abinay Chaturvedi was an extremely astute and smart officer. True to his name, he lived by a code of conduct, he believed he was a protector of everyone around him, a guardian of humanity. He came across as a man with an attitude that made him trust that his destiny was to be the shield to anyone who could be in trouble and needed help, irrespective of the past they had.

His dutiful nature was due to one very strong reason, which was also why he had chosen his profession. Apart from his belief and innate nature, the training, the experiences he had undergone and an inquisitive mind that never agreed to quit unless his curiosity was satisfied played a major role.

Popularly known as Agent Hawk for his keen observation and intelligence, Abinay had a proven track record. He was one of the most feared in the dark world of crime. He rose in prominence after famously nabbing one of the masterminds of the Indian Mujahedeen, the terror outfit that was allegedly sponsored by Lashkar-e-Taiba in 2008.

He had no doubt in his mind that the scientist was killed. Something told him it was not just a cold-blooded murder. It seemed like something very mysterious. Something that would take him deep into a new mystery.

Abinay sent the scientist's dead body for postmortem and put the forensic experts to work. They were asked to collect every bit of sample they could find, which could help him to find the murderer.

The forensics closely and carefully worked to take samples of the fingerprints from the glass Yuyutsu drank his whisky in. They also took samples of the alcohol he was drinking. Agent Hawk summoned the waiter who was serving the deceased.

"Tell me boy, wasn't it you who murdered this man? Why did you do it?" asked the inspector in a voice as cold and smooth as ice.

Listening to the officer, the waiter felt as nervous as a cat on a hot tin roof. He did not know how to react. He plummeted to the inspector's feet and begged him.

The waiter said in a trembling voice, "Sir, please trust me... I did not do anything. I am not responsible for the guest's death. I was only doing my job, and that was to serve the guest in the best way possible."

"You were the only one here when the man died. Then why isn't it possible that you might have killed him? And then you rushed to your manager to report his condition to use that as an alibi."

"No sir, believe me. I only brought him the drink he asked for."

"Was the bottle open before you served the drink to him?"

"No sir, but as a gesture to the guest, I had made the drink for him before I came to the suite."

"You made the drink before you entered the suite, did you?" How stupid could you be?" Abinay shouted furiously, hitting his palm to his forehead. He stormed out of the suite at once to see the manager of the hotel.

"I need to see the recording of CCTV closest to the guest's suite, at once!"

"Yes officer, of course. I shall get that arranged right away. We have a CCTV camera in every corridor, every floor. Coincidentally, the camera on the guest's floor is right outside the suite in question."

The manager immediately called the head of security and asked him to retrieve the visuals requested by the cop. As the officer watched the recording very carefully, he saw the waiter emerge with the quarter filled glass and an unopened single malt whisky bottle on a tray over his shoulder.

He stood outside the suite, waiting to be allowed to enter. That is where Abinay paused the recording. He replayed it multiple times, back and forth. He watched a particular bit in ultra-slow motion several times. He had certainly noticed something, so he ran towards the scientist's suite.

The manager followed him, "What are you looking for officcr?"

"The CCTV camera."

"It's on the pillar beside the scientist's suite."

Abinay rushed to the point and stared at the camera posted on it for a long moment.

"How on earth..."

"What happened, officer? What is it that confuses you?"

The manager asked watching the confused look on Abinay's face.

"How on earth could anyone pop in that tablet into the glass from such a distance... so accurately? At least 15-18 feet..." he mumbled. Then he turned to the manager and said, "I am leaving for now, but I will return whenever it is required. However, two constables will keep a watch on the hotel while they stay here. This floor will remain inaccessible to everyone except us, till we finish the investigation. Even if a soul steps in here without my knowledge, I will not spare you."

▼

As Abinay sat in his cabin at the police headquarters of Bangalore, staring at the postmortem report of the dead scientist, the phone at his desk sprang to life, ringing aloud. In a hoarse voice, the IG police spoke, "Officer Abinay!"

"Yes sir."

"I am banking on you to crack this case as soon as possible. A scientist the world celebrated has allegedly been killed in our city in mysterious circumstances. There is enormous pressure on the department, the world is watching us. If we don't nab the culprit soon and if any other agencies step in, it will be an insult to the police department. I don't want such a thing to happen and you must make sure of it."

"I will not let you down, sir. I'll make sure we put the culprit behind bars."

Abinay took a moment, pepped himself on! And then stuck his face back into the chemical report on the last few drops of whisky that were found in the glass and the whisky in the bottle. As expected, the alcohol in the bottle was clean, which meant the killer was very sure that the few crystals of poison he somehow threw in the open glass were potent enough to kill the victim.

The postmortem report declared that death was due to the continued migration of sodium ions in cells of muscles and nerves, causing a heart failure.

However, the report showed the presence of a very rare venom called Batrachotoxin in the remains of the glass. The postmortem report also read, *Traces of Batrachotoxin found in the body, that jams sodium ions in the cells of muscles and nerves, hence causing a heart failure.*

Abinay, immediately turned to his laptop screen, to google Batrachotoxin. The search engine read,

> *Batrachotoxin is one of the most potent toxins, extracted from wild frogs found in South America, the lethal dose of which is two mg of every kilogram. That would mean an amount of 2-3 salt grains can kill someone in a matter of minutes.*

That's when a junior officer Lance, a half-African by birth walked in. His father was Indian and mother was from Africa. He had inherited his physical attributes from his maternal family – tall, dark and a well-built physique, literally a giant! Having spent his formative years in the core of Africa, he was aware of quite a few of the tribal practices of that country. He respected Abinay and looked up to him as a role model.

In fact, Abinay was the reason why Lance had chosen to become a cop himself. As a teenager in Delhi, he was immensely inspired by the way his role model nabbed the terror-mongers and anti-social elements. He was impacted even more by how Abinay fought against the system, being a part of it, right the wrong that would have happened to him and his team. Reading about him and following his deeds, his leadership skill motivated young Lance.

Abinay was seldom seen perplexed, even in the most traumatic of situations. But something about the scientist's death troubled him.

"What is the matter, chief? You look deeply concerned. Can I help?"

Abinay handed Lance the blow gun that he had ordered online and asked him to show him the use of the instrument.

"Look at this Lance, I guess you know what this is."

Lance took the object in his hand, examined it for a while and then said, "Chief, the blow gun is a simple ranged weapon used to propel light projectiles like darts by blowing into it. But why do you ask?"

"Watch the recording from the hotel, Lance. See, this was recorded before Yuyutsu Ghosh died," Abinay said, scrolling through the video and showing Lance the point where he had noticed something fishy. He continued, "My gut feel says these tiny tablets, the cause for the scientist's death, were catapulted into the whisky glass using this kind of a blow gun. Otherwise such an accuracy from such a distance is improbable.

"The best of blow gun shooters can shoot a maximum distance of ten feet. But the distance here is much more than that!

"Also, I suppose the angle at which the pills got popped into the crystal glass, they couldn't be thrown into the glass from any other place but the top of the staircase. Because it is highly unlikely that such pinpoint accuracy could be achieved otherwise."

"Chief, you might be right in saying a blow gun could be used, but it definitely cannot be one of these available in the market. It surely would be a customized blow gun, because these tablets are way too small to be accurately blown by one of these things."

Abinay nodded, but Lance asked further, "What about the arrow we found?"

Abinay inhaled deeply and nodding his head, projected an image from his laptop on the screen in his office.

"What is this engraved on the arrow? It seems so weird! I have never seen a tattooed arrow before," Abinay said.

Lance said shrugging his shoulders, "The thing that intrigues me is how it reached the scientist's suite. The arrow was shot from the terrace of the opposite building, using a compound bow. Strangely enough, it had been left there for us to find it."

"What makes the scenario more baffling is that the arrow was shot at an angle precisely. Because of which it got stuck exactly at the feet of Lord Buddha's portrait. It was shot not an inch above, not an inch below. Why would anyone leave a compound bow for us to find and shoot an arrow at the feet of a portrait?" Abinay said.

"Chief, I guess the answers to all your questions lie in the image engraved on the arrowhead. We need to find out everything about it, that is our only chance!"

"You are right, Lance, I must find a way to explore more about the engraved image. But the image being engraved on the arrowhead could just be a coincidence. All that we are thinking may only be our imagination. This could be a crime like any other crime in the city."

Abinay continued to stare at the arrowhead projected on the screen. Both men were lost in deep thought, when a constable knocked at the door as if he was at the entry to a lion's den!

"Yes…"

The constable timidly stepped inside the cabin.

"Sir, there is a lady outside who wants to see you, may I let her in to meet you?"

"Is it something you folks cannot help her with? Does she want to escalate something about one of you guys to me?"

The constable was well aware of the chief's anger, "No sir! The lady says she has some vital information related to the scientist's death. She saw the news about the alleged death and came to report something. I thought it's best she speaks to you."

"Okay, ask her to come in."

Abinay signalled Lance to be alert and attentive, as this could be the breakthrough they were after. Both men sat upright, not knowing what to expect. Abinay and Lance were staring at the screen which still displayed the image of the arrow, trying to make sense out of the engraving on its head. As the lady entered the cabin, the two cops were up on their feet, a mark of respect to the woman. Something Anvesha had not expected… cops up on their feet in respect of a civilian, that too a woman.

"Please have a seat ma'am, and tell me who are you and what is that you wish to tell me about the scientist's death?"

Looking at his badge, she began, "Officer Abinay, my name is Anvesha Roy. I learnt about the scientist's death from the news channels, the arrow, and the curious engraving on it was also described in the piece. The description of the engraved image forced me to take notice of the incident and made me come here."

"What about it? Do you know anything related to it?"

"Is this the same arrow, officer?"Anvesha asked looking at the screen.

"Yes, it is"

"The image!"

"Yes, what about it?"

Anvesha walked up to the screen and gazed at the engraved image for a long moment. Then she spoke, "Officer, there isn't any written record in history that has been archived. But I am trying to join a few dots to identify a larger picture. My speculation could be entirely wrong, but it is not baseless. You are trying to understand this image as a whole, try looking at it in separate pieces. Then you may be able to make sense of what I am going to say.

"You see, in Buddhism, *dharma* or righteousness is represented by the wheel. Popularly known as the *Dharmachakra*, the wheel of righteousness. According to Buddhist teachings, a wheel represents righteousness, because a circle or round is as perfect as dharma itself. The wheel is depicted with different number of spokes and it represents different concepts depending on the number of spokes it has.

"The most commonly seen wheel is with eight spokes, denoting the eight-fold path. The eight paths that define dharma are:

- ✦ View
- ✦ Intention
- ✦ Speech
- ✦ Action
- ✦ Livelihood
- ✦ Mindfulness
- ✦ Effort
- ✦ Concentration

"If the wheel has ten spokes, then the spokes represent the ten directions. The other very relatable form of the dharmachakra is the Ashoka Chakra on the national flag with twenty-four spokes. Twelve of which represent the links of dependent origination.

"The other twelve spokes in the Ashoka Chakra are the reversals of the first twelve. According to this principle, everything happens as a cause or effect of something, which means everything that happens is interrelated.

"If you notice officer, this principle resembles Newton's third law of motion. It states that every action has an equal and opposite reaction. Buddhism originated in India roughly 1400 years before Newton was born. Spiritual science is much advanced than all the modern scientific advancements. But unfortunately, we Indians fail to understand the simple fact."

Both Abinay and Lance were listening to Anvesha, but at the back of their minds, they were thinking how all this was connected to the scientist's death. Hence Abinay asked, "I understand and appreciate the depth of your knowledge ma'am, but if you notice the wheel in the image on the arrowhead, it has nine spokes. You never spoke of nine spokes. I wonder if you are thinking in the right direction. No offence ma'am, but I think you are connecting two entirely different threads."

"No officer, I was about to come to your point of nine spokes in the wheel. Just hear me out and you will realize the connection, I am referring to.

"As I told you, the Dharmachakra has 4, 8, 10, 12 or 24 spokes, but a wheel with nine spokes is nowhere mentioned in recorded history. These nine spokes might be referring to the secret society of nine people, which was formed by Ashoka the great. The objective of such an elusive group was to build the greatest of knowledge bases. Then use it to guide the society to live by the code of conduct, which is Dharma.

"It could be possible that these nine spokes are pointing to that secret society. It may be imbibed in the wheel because the purpose of the society was to protect righteousness. As far as the lion face in the center is concerned, you might very well know that the lion was part of Ashoka's emblem. The Indian emblem is also inspired from the Mauryan Empire."

Anvesha's eyes twinkled in nervous energy, as she wasn't sure if Abinay and Lance were convinced with her description. There was pin drop silence in the room. The historian did not know what to expect! Both men were trying to comprehend what they had heard and make sense out of it. After a long moment of silence, Agent Hawk rose to his feet and walking a few paces, said, "Ma'am, are you suggesting that an organization or set of nine people, who you say is a two thousand-year-old secret society is behind this murder? No offence madam, but as you yourself said, there is no written record or any other kind of proof of the existence of this organization. Don't you think if we go behind someone we are not even sure exists, we will be chasing a wild goose?"

"I am not suggesting anything, officer. As a responsible citizen of the city, I only wanted to share information that I thought could help. As a research scholar, the things I tried to give you, is only my perspective. You will be a better judge of if it adds any value to your investigation. If you think I wasted your precious time, I am extremely sorry. I only wanted to help."

Abinay sensed the spunk and the sarcasm in the response from Anvesha. He was well aware of the kind of reputation his department had. Despite such a bad image, she had made a conscious effort to fulfill her duty as a citizen. He realized that he better appreciate the lady's sense of responsibility and commitment. Without wasting any time, the cop responded, "Ma'am, please do not get me wrong, I had no intent of offending you. All I meant was it is difficult to believe that there is a secret society that could be nothing but a fantasy. This seems like a far-fetched idea. But there is no doubt about my respect for you and your dutiful attitude. I would reach out to you if I need help. Please leave your contact details with my team. Please do not share these details in public; it might set the city in panic. Thank you very much."

After Anvesha left the headquarters, Abinay told Lance, "Make sure everything that was discussed here doesn't reach the media. Even if it does, make sure it isn't published. I don't want the city to panic imagining unnecessary things. Also keep an eye on our visitor."

Lance nodded in affirmative and walked out of the cabin. Abinay picked his phone and called Dr Pashupathi, the forensic expert who had done the postmortem of Yuyutsu's dead body.

"Doctor, did you find the details I asked you for?"

"You mean data on the venom that killed the scientist, Batrachotoxin?"

"Yes."

"Yes officer, I have done some research about the venom and I do have information you would want to know."

"Alright doctor, I am on my way to see you."

Thirty minutes later, the cop and the doctor were sitting next to each other. The two men were literal opposites when it came to physiques. The cop was fit as a fiddle, while the doctor was not only short and stout, his head shone like the full moon, as he had lost all the hair except at the back of his head. He was more or less the modern version of Hardy, the comic character. But he was a master in his work. Dr Pashupathi described the identified poison.

"Batrachotoxin, as you might already know, in this case obtained from Golden Poison Frog is extremely rare and potent as it is found in a very tiny and most attractive species of frogs, in the woods of South American countries like Columbia, Brazil, Costa Rica. The creature grows to a length of 1.5 inches. Though considered one of the most adorable animals to look at, this tiny animal is one of the deadliest too. One golden poison frog contains enough venom to kill ten grown-up humans.

"These frogs belong to a larger family of poison frogs called Dendrobatidae, which has over 170 species." As Dr Pashupathi continued to speak, Abinay interrupted him,

"Just because these tiny frogs are found in the South American wild, does it make the poison they make rare?"

There were questions written all over the cop's face, accepting anything without darting questions was neither in his nature, nor in his training. Not believing even the obvious without investigating was the thumb rule he always followed.

But often his interrogating questions offended his audience, no matter if they had a criminal background or not. But not Dr Pashupathi, for he had been working in the forensic department for long enough to know how things worked in the judicial system. Moreover, he knew Abinay well enough to understand that his intention was only to find the truth. A bit of banter between the two men was mutually well received.

"Officer, I know my job pretty well and what I am telling you is based on scientific research. Yes, Batrachotoxin is a rare kind of venom, because the golden poison frogs live in the Amazon forest. The toxin found in these amphibians is a kind of alkaloid and alkaloids are nitrogen containing bases. These alkaloids have diverse physiological effects on humans, and animals too.

"Scientists have debated for long about the source of the poison. But clinical research has proven that Batrachotoxin is exogenous, meaning it is not synthesized by the frog on its own like a snake. These frogs are not venomous by birth. Instead, they obtain and concentrate the toxin from their diet. This process is technically called Diet-toxicity Hypothesis.

"Ants and small arthropods that eat plants which are the ultimate source of alkaloids, form most of the frog's diet. The theory is furthermore supported by the fact that the frogs of the same species, if raised in captivity, do not develop their poison because their diet is controlled.

"But in the wild the venom from the creature will be deadly. Even if a small quantity of the toxin enters your body through a cut on your skin or any other way, it would be fatal."

A look of dissatisfaction still loomed large on Abinay's face. He was about to pose his next question, but this time he was cut short, "I know what you are thinking officer; your next question to me is, if it is true that these frog's poison really comes from what they eat then how do they themselves survive the toxin? Isn't it? In fact it is a very intelligent question, my dear friend. Don't worry! I shall quench your curiosity. But before that, you need to understand how the toxin actually works.

"Batrachotoxin works by irreversibly opening the sodium channels of nerve cells in the body. Hence blocking the nerve signals from reaching the muscles and disabling them from relaxing. The heart is a muscle too and is susceptible to the toxin and could lead to a cardiac failure. If you have read and remember the postmortem report, the scientist Yuyutsu Ghosh died of cardiac failure.

"That is the very reason why the Choco tribe of Columbia, also known as the Embera Indians, have found through their experience in the wild that these frogs, when impaled and exposed to heat, sweat the poison out. This poison is used by the tribe to coat their weapons for hunting larger prey.

"Now to understand why are the frogs immune to such a rare and potent toxin? Do you know what amino acids are? Amino acids are organic compounds that majorly contains oxygen, hydrogen, carbon and nitrogen. Research has shown, the reason behind the frog's immunity is the presence of an amino acid that is resistant to the effect of the venom."

Dr Pashupathi had just finished and Abinay was waiting with a frown on his forehead and his next question.

"In that case, do these animals have no threats?"

The forensic expert breathed out a sad sigh and then spoke again, "Due to their toxicity, it is true that these tiny creatures have only one natural predator. That is the Fire-bellied snake, which has developed resistance to Batrachotoxin. But this doesn't mean these frogs are a thriving species; many poison dart frog species are facing a steep decline in their numbers. Some even have been classified as endangered, due to the constant loss of the rain forest habitat."

"You said a snake has developed resistance to the frog's toxin; does that mean an antidote has been developed?"

"Unfortunately, no! Scientists across the globe haven't yet found success in making the antidote for Batrachotoxin. But yes, the scientific community has successfully replicated the venom artificially in twenty-four complex steps. Along with it they also created mirror images of the same molecule. Onc molecule worked as a cure to morning sickness in pregnant women, the other resulted in birth defects."

Finally, all the questions about the deadly toxin in the cop's mind were put to rest. But the road map ahead was still hazy. Abinay wasn't clear what the next step in his investigation must be. Though it seemed like he was shooting in the dark and he had nothing to aim at, Abinay very well knew that the killer was teasing the entire system, and the police department in particular. In a way, the culprit was throwing an open challenge to find him. However, Abinay wasn't someone to quit.

His experience as a crime investigator over the years had taught him that modern crime and criminals have grown smart enough to outfox the traditional methodologies of investigation and he too would have to use modern technology to fight back. He knew he had to get the digital forces at work.

Abinay asked his team to contact the telecom service providers and retrieve the dead scientist's call detail records (CDRs) for further analysis. Since this was a high-profile case, Abinay himself wrote a note to the head of the cybercrime team to get his best team working on it, on priority.

After a few days, Manish Sharma from the cybercrime cell visited Abinay's office. He was middle-aged, probably in his late forties with a common personality of any IT professional, a tinge of salt in his beard. His keen eyes hinted at how observant he was. Abinay was very sure there wouldn't be any detail that those keen eyes would miss.

"Tell me Manish, I have been looking forward to see you since I received your boss's e-mail last night. Your mail says that your team hasn't found anything that looked dubious. Could you please elaborate on it?"

"Yes Abinay, we have not found any thing doubtful in Yuyutsu Ghosh's CDR. Most people who called him in the past six months or whom the scientist called were known to him. The rest were not those one would worry from a security point of view."

"But how is that possible? I am sure the killer or someone related to him would have certainly tried getting in touch with Yuyutsu. The scientist seems to be old-fashioned. I checked his mobile device; he hasn't installed any chat applications like WhatsApp. He is not on social media too, I searched for him on Facebook, Twitter and Instagram.

"Though there is a possibility that he might be having all his communication through e-mails. But I am sure somehow, somewhere that the protocol would have been broken at least once, because not everyone he used to communicate with would follow the protocol. As far as I know, every call made from or to a mobile device can be tracked. Then how is it that you are not able to find anything on Yuyutsu's phone?"

"You are right Abinay, every call made from or to a mobile device does reflect in the CDR. But there is a distinct possibility that if these calls were not made using an actual phone but specific internet applications, they are very difficult to trace, if not impossible."

Abinay seemed confused. Not knowing what to question, he was keen to listen. Manish understood his confusion and continued, "I'll explain what I am trying to tell you, my friend. Service providers can trace calls and fetch call detail records if the call goes through a local operator. Every single detail of your private life can be found out through your mobile. Think about it, we willingly provide information by logging into Facebook or providing email IDs and phone numbers.

"Much can be revealed just from your phone bill, but tracking becomes a different ball game when advanced technology calls the shots in the game. In most situations, calls get routed and scrambled through two different servers and providers.

"Once the call gets through, it gets connected through a secure data connection to maximize privacy for both ends of the call. This means you can make calls without leaving any trace on the recipient's device. What might make a few applications even more secure is that they give you the option of deleting the cookies. Hence personal information cannot be rented or sold to third parties.

"This also means the vendors protect your information from themselves too. They don't track any information during the call, the duration, the destination, not even the device you use."

Manish continued while Abinay listened with paramount keenness, "You might remember the chaos that happened a while ago in the government bodies regarding privacy laws? The lack of understanding of cyber privacy laws for so long in India has led to a lot grey area in the efforts of putting strong rules in place. In the interest of the sovereignty and integrity of India, intercepts can be of people including their computer resource only with the authorization of the Home Ministry."

"That was going to be my next question, Manish. I was thinking, as we have not found anything dubious on Yuyutsu's phone, I was wondering if we could find something on his computer?"

Manish tried to remind something to his colleague to which Abinay interrupted, "I'll get you all the permissions you need. And you get into that damn machine and find out what is hidden in it."

"That I know you will Abinay, but that isn't what I was proposing. After looking at Yuyutsu's phone, I doubt if we can find anything on his laptop. I suggest we search his home and his bank or other security lockers for memory devices. It is my strong suspicion that we will find some vital leads in those devices, if there are any."

"Don't worry, I'll get you all that you need, you make sure you find the leads. I need to find the culprits and put them behind bars."

▼

Two weeks had passed since Yuyutsu's death. Abinay's superiors had not seen much progress made. The pressure on the department was increasing every day and in turn on Abinay. But the pressure of expectation from himself was no less on him.

Soon the requisition to search Yuyutsu's belongings was put forth to the Home Ministry. No surprises for guessing the request was considered and the permission granted. Even the authorities wanted to dig the truth behind the sudden and suspicious death of the scientist.

In the next few days, the police led by Abinay had collected Yuyutsu's bank details from the ISA. The team was puzzled to learn from the ISA that Yuyutsu had resigned from the organization. They also had secured a search warrant to search the dead scientist's house.

The address was of an old apartment building and there was nothing fancy about it. The walls looked pale from the outside, the paint had all but come off and railings in the staircase had reached their expiry date.

But the investigating team had no option but to take the stairs as the lift did not look healthy and strong enough to even carry three people and made cranky noises as it reluctantly opened its door. The staircase led to a corridor of three houses. The name plate on the door of the house at the end of the pathway read Yuyutsu Ghosh.

Abinay walked up to the door, leading his team. In a couple of minutes after he rang the bell, the door opened. The interior of the house was dark, much like the moods of the people living in it. At the door stood a middle-aged woman with a gloomy face, but seeing the cops at her doorstep, she felt the ground slip away from under her feet. For a moment, her mouth went dry. Abinay sensed it, and was grateful she let them in.

"Ma'am, you need not panic! We know you are hurt, but we need your help. We are here because we need help from you to find out who killed Mr Yuyutsu Ghosh. We need you to tell us what kind of a person he was? Did he have any enemies? Do you suspect anyone in his killing?"

The lady regained her composure soon and with a steely determination in her eyes, she said, "Come in officer. Yes, I am hurt but will extend all the support I can. I want the killer of my brother as soon as possible. You must bring the guilty to justice at any cost!"

Then she started narrating more about her brother, "Yuyutsu was a man of very few words, he would always be at his lab. He would only come home once in a week. Then also he would be glued to his laptop or drown himself in books or his research papers. His research was everything to him, his ambition of making his mark in space research was his life goal. Hence, he could never have a family life. I, being his sister, am the only family he was left with."

"Did you notice anything strange in his behavior of late?"

There was a sudden anxiety in the woman's expression. Abinay bent forward to listen to her.

"From a very long time, my brother was angry and disappointed about not being able to get the attention of his superiors towards the research he was pursuing. Things had gone from bad to worse after he was insulted."

"Wait a minute, Yuyutsu was insulted? How?"

"He had some project proposal, but none of his colleagues realized his worth and ridiculed him. My brother was a genius himself, he didn't need to steal ideas from anyone.

"But recently, one day he came and told me, someone finally found the worth of the hard work he had put in for years! Somebody had finally arrived like the jeweller who knows the worth of the precious jewel he was. He sounded very excited that day. That is the last I heard from him."

"Did you know that your brother had resigned from ISA?"

The woman shook her head in a negative.

"Do you know what kind of research Yuyutsu was doing?"

"No, I don't. I don't understand the kind of high profile work he did. However, he never shared anything about his work with anyone. He kept it to himself. But you know what officer, I am not surprised at my brother's resignation. I think he had finally got something he truly deserved."

"Can we take a look at his belongings?"

The lady nodded and led the team to Yuyutsu's room, that was in a total mess. There was no space even to step inside. It was a sea of fat, big books. As he fiddled in the cupboards, everything that he could lay his hands on was related to astronomy and space research. Nothing Abinay saw made any sense to him. But his eyes were looking for something that could lead his investigation in the right direction.

Abinay could not find anything that he felt could be dubious, until he found a story book.

"Would a scientist like Yuyutsu really be interested in reading story books?"

It did not seem likely and made the cop scurry through the book. As he did so, he found a few pages stuck together with glue. This triggered the curiosity in him, and he began to look closely. The middle pages were cut through the centre. He noticed something hidden in those cut pages. It was a key. Abinay's eyes lit up in anticipation.

"Ma'am do you know what key this is?"

The woman replied in a negative and the team could not find anything more that would have proved useful in the investigation. Abinay recovered all the bank passbooks that they could find in the house to figure out which bank the key they had found belonged to. But Abinay noticed a surprised look on the lady's face when he had asked her about the key.

He chose not to question her, but he was sure Yuyutsu's sister did not know about the key. Her reaction made it clear to him that she was as surprised as he himself to find the key hidden in a story book.

In couple of hours, Abinay had information of the bank and the branch where the locker was. In the next thirty minutes, Abinay was at the branch manager's desk, interrogating him.

"Sir, I am the investigating officer of the high-profile ISA scientist murder case that shook the city recently. My name is Abinay, here is my ID card and this is the key of one of the lockers in your bank. I expect you and your staff would co-operate in our investigation."

The bank manager was taken aback for a moment; he did not know how to respond. He had never been in such a situation, he and felt quite intimidated being in the presence of a police officer. He tried swallowing his fear and being normal, but his emotions were quite evident on his face. In response to Abinay, the manager could only manage to nod meekly in the affirmative.

"Please examine this key and confirm if it belongs to one of the lockers in your custody." The manager nodded and took the key to look at it.

"Yes officer, you are right! This key belongs to our bank."

"Who does the locker belong to?"

"I'll have to check, give me a minute, officer."

The manager called the clerk to come into his cabin immediately.

"Look at this key, it belongs to one of our customers. Please find out immediately who does it belong to!"

"Yes sir, I will get you the information right away."

Abinay noticed the nervousness in both the clerk and his boss.

"Don't be afraid of us gentlemen, we are public servants. Our intention is never to harass the innocent but only punish the guilty. If you have done nothing wrong, you need not fear. Rather, you must help us."

The clerk grinned reluctantly and rushed to his computer to get the information he was asked for. He returned in a few minutes with a concerned look on his face.

"What happened? Why has the blood drained off your face? Whose locker is it?"

"I have sent the account details to your computer already sir. Please have a look, you will realize yourself!"

The manager unlocked his computer and clicked on the notification that had popped up on his screen. The next moment, he seemed as stunned as his subordinate standing next to him.

"Are you sure about this?"

The clerk nodded hesitantly, looking at both the flabbergasted faces. Abinay turned the computer monitor towards himself and the grin gradually widened.

"Officer, is this the same scientist who was killed recently?"

"Yes, Mr Manager! We have very strong doubts that this is the same Yuyutsu Ghosh, who was allegedly killed a few weeks ago. That is what we are here to confirm as part of our investigation."

Suddenly the grin on Abinay's face vanished and got replaced by a stern look.

"I need to see all the transaction details that were done through this account and any other account linked to it. Meanwhile, let us go and check out what is hidden in the locker."

The clerk hurried back to his computer, as both the bank manager and Abinay walked towards the locker room. They walked into a narrow passage that led to a room, guarded by weapon-enabled guards. From the outside, Abinay could see just iron doors and concrete walls, within which there were hundreds of boxes, and one of them contained Yuyutsu's belongings.

The manager still felt jittery walking beside the cop, as if he was walking on broken glass. To make things worse, Abinay continued the questioning,

"Has Yuyutsu owned this locker for long?"

Swallowing his discomfort, the manager spoke, "No officer. Though he has had an account with us for years, he never rented a locker. I had asked him many times over the years to rent a locker as it would help the bank's business. But he never obliged until recently when he himself came to the branch asking for a locker to be rented. I even ridiculed him that day saying had he suddenly found a treasure that he wanted to protect."

"What makes you remember this conversation so vividly? You might meet many customers every day."

"Yes, I do officer, but I remember this meeting very clearly because Mr Yuyutsu seemed quite unlike himself that day."

"What do you mean by unlike himself?" Abinay asked narrowing his eyes and closing in on the manager, sending a chill down his spine.

"Mr Yuyutsu had always seemed like a confident personality to me, but that day, he looked very fidgety. He was sweating, seemed very uncomfortable and restless. I did not want to bother him much, so I did not push him. Moreover, it is the customer's right to maintain complete secrecy about what he wants to keep in the locker. It is our duty to let him maintain privacy."

As Abinay walked through the narrow passage to reach the entrance of the locker room, he wondered, 'What might have transpired that the scientist suddenly rented a locker for himself? What has he hidden in the locker?'

By the time both the men had finished the conversation, they had entered the locker room. Before the bank manager left, he turned in the bank's key for Yuyutsu's locker and asked Abinay to turn in the key in his possession. Once Abinay was alone, he unlocked the locker. It was a long narrow box in which was a tiny rectangular-shaped device.

Abinay took it out to see that it was a hard disk. He wondered, 'Why would a scientist like Yuyutsu hide a memory device in his bank locker? What confidential information did he possess? Was the information he possessed the reason for his death? I hope the cybercrime people can get some information to lead me further in my investigation. But I need to dig through his life, probably that would lead me in the right direction.'

Abinay took possession of the disk, returned to his office to plug the disk into his computer and see what the precious data was that the scientist had so carefully protected. He found out that Yuyutsu had not stopped at keeping the disk in the bank locker. He had encrypted it. A deep frown curved on his forehead.

"What kind of secret was Yuyutsu trying to guard? If he was protecting any data related to ISA, he couldn't be keeping it in his possession, even if he had an official approval to keep it. He would have returned it when he resigned from the organization, but that did not happen. If it was a family secret, his sister must have known about it. There definitely is something fishy in that hard disk."

He immediately wrote an email to the cybercrime chief Manish Sharma, letting him know that a package containing a hard disk that was recovered from Yuyutsu's belongings would be sent to him. The hard disk could contain vital information about the scientist and his death.

Abinay had sent the email and was contemplating his next move when Lance entered. Though he was engrossed in his thoughts, he noticed Lance and signalled him to take a seat.

"Chief!"

"Lance, did you find out why Yuyutsu was arrested?"

"Yes Chief, his sister was right. It was a charge of IP theft. But as expected, back in those years, our legal system did not have strong laws against such cases. Neither the investigation was done convincingly enough. I couldn't gather much as the complaint was withdrawn. But I have something to show you. This could be related to Yuyutsu's murder case."

There was a sudden alarm in Abinay's eyes and he sat up.

"What is it Lance? Tell me about it!"

There was immense intensity and excitement in his voice.

"Chief, you remember what I had told you about your blowgun theory?"

"Yes, I do, you had said that such accuracy in shooting the venom-soaked grains could be achieved in a customized tool."

"Exactly! I have found something similar, a unique toy. It is possible that our culprit used something similar."

"What makes you so confident Lance? Could you elaborate?"

Lance was about to continue when the conversation was interrupted with Abinay's mobile phone ringing. He saw the cybercrime chief's name flash on the screen and wasted no time in receiving the call.

"Yes Manish, tell me. Did you receive the package I sent to you?"

"Yes, I did. I will work on the disk and as soon as I make any breakthrough, I will reach out to you with the updates."

The line went dead and Abinay focused back to what Lance had to say. By then Lance was ready to play a video on the internet that had been titled *the soda bottle gun*. The video began with making a hole large enough for a plastic straw to be inserted through the cap of a plastic soda bottle. The straw was tightly stuck to the cap and the bottle was closed. Then a similar hole was made towards the bottom of the bottle, in which the tail end of the plastic straw was inserted.

A container piece of a syringe was attached to the bottle that would act as a handle to the gun. The remaining end of the pipe was then connected to a deodorant spray. In the end, the soda was filled with tiny balls. Each time the sprayer blew out air, the tiny balls were triggered out like bullets from the straw at the mouth of the bottle.

The video ended as the two men looked at each other.

"What you are saying makes sense Lance, the tiny balls in the video are roughly of the same size as the poisonous grains I noticed in the CCTV footage. The question that remains now is, if the toy can fire projectiles as far as ten feet? That too seems possible if a more powerful mechanism is used to trigger the balls."

As Abinay posed the question, he noticed a spark in his subordinate's eyes. A sense of achievement and pride was evident in the grin that grew wider. Lance was quietly confident that his boss would like what he was about to tell him. The look on Lance's face was something that made Abinay happy.

"My sources have brought information about an artisan who makes toys for a living. I am pretty confident he will have something important to tell us. I had asked my informers to keep an eye on all toy sellers in town and find out if they have had any customer who bought any such toy. I have been informed that this guy sold a unique toy gun recently."

"That is great news, Lance. Let us follow this lead. We don't have time to waste. Also share his contact details with me."

In the next thirty minutes, Abinay and Lance were in a narrow crowded street, dressed in casuals. Every spot in the street had a big, small or micro shop in which customers had piled up like bees in a hive. It was nothing less than chaos, to say the least. Both men were dressed in casuals, so the shopkeeper was extremely busy in attending to customers.

Lance sneaked his way to the shopkeeper and quietly popped his identity card to him, making sure no customer noticed it. The shopkeeper was shell-shocked to see a cop visit him at his shop. Not knowing why the cops had come for him, his heart had come to his mouth. Without realizing, the shopkeeper's mouth went dry. Moments later he saw his phone screen flash with an unknown number. With sweaty palms, he received the call, to hear a deep voice from the other end.

"Listen to me very carefully, this is the police, and I am ACP Abinay. The man who showed his identity card to you is officer Lance, my subordinate. Now just do as you are told to. Get rid of your customers in the next five minutes, shut the front door of the shop and let me and my men in from the back door."

The line went dead before the shopkeeper could respond, the authority and conviction in the instructions made the listener tremble! In sudden shock, he dropped his phone to the ground, he felt his knees go weak. His mind went blank and he started to act as instructed mechanically.

Watching the shopkeeper's reaction, a sly smile appeared on Lance's usually serious face. It wasn't the first time someone had reacted to Abinay like this. Lance had seen Abinay interrogate many suspects. He hardly used cruel methods of punishments for confessions to seasoned criminals. Smart enough to make them spit the truth without using violence. The shopkeeper was no match to the ACP and hence Lance wasn't surprised a bit in the way he reacted.

The shopkeeper hurriedly and abruptly asked the customers to leave as he had to attend to a family emergency and must shut the shop immediately and leave. A few customers were annoyed at this weird behaviour of the shopkeeper.

In the next five minutes, the shop was shut and there were only three people inside; two of whom were prowling tigers in the guise of cops. The two men circled around the shopkeeper as if he was their meek prey. Trembling, as if he had seen a ghost, he asked, "Sir, what wrong have I done that officers like you have come looking for me?"

Abinay suddenly stopped and looked directly into the man's eyes, sending a chill down his spine.

"You are saying that you have no idea why we are here, right? But for us you are our prime suspect of the murder that shook the city a few weeks ago. Now you are under arrest for the same.

The shopkeeper felt as if he was stung by a scorpion. He was literally in shambles. His world had turned upside down in a matter of minutes. He was selling toys busily minutes ago and within no time he had become a prime suspect of a high-profile murder case. He had no idea about what the cop in front of him was talking about.

"Sir, believe me, I am innocent, I haven't committed any crime! I am a poor man fighting a battle of survival daily. Why will I kill anyone? Please trust me sir, I have no motive to do so."

A sinister smile surfaced on Abinay's face. "You want me to believe what you are telling me? You think I am a fool! Do you?"

Abinay bent over on the shopkeeper's face, so close that he could feel the cop's breath.

"As per our investigation, the toy like the one that was used as the weapon in the murder of the scientist was seen in your shop, hence the suspicion on you."

The shopkeeper saw in Abinay a keen hawk vigilantly watching a potential prey. One wrong move and he would be torn to pieces. The shopkeeper trembled like an animal looking for a burrow to hide from the claws of death itself, but could not find any. The shopkeeper quivered to the cops who held him hostage in his own shop, "Sir, please believe me! I am innocent, I am not guilty of any crime, please let me go."

Abinay looked around the small shop, scanning every nook and corner with his eyes. Strangely enough for him, he couldn't find anything like the toy gun he was looking for. Both Lance and the shopkeeper looked at each other in a perplexed manner. While Abinay scratched his stubble subtly, narrowing his eyes and deepening the curves on his forehead, he gazed at the shopkeeper for a long moment, which seemed endless to him.

Then taking out his phone, he looked for the toy making video that had brought them to the shop in the first place.

He played it and asked the shopkeeper, if he recognized anything like it; the shopkeeper nodded hastily.

He sought for words to say something. But fear made him feel choked and he could hardly speak. He literally curled up in front of the police officer. Lanced looked at Abinay, on whose cue he offered the shopkeeper some water from the can in the shop.

He grabbed it and gulped all that he could, and when after a couple of minutes, he had caught his breath, he spoke, "Yes sir, I built a very similar toy to the one in this video. But not for my use. I was asked to make it by a customer. He offered me a hefty amount for the kind of effort the making of the toy required. The money he offered me lured me into making what he needed. I did not reason out on the purpose of the tool."

Both listeners' eyes lit up the moment they heard that someone had asked to make the toy gun.

"Who asked you to make such a toy? Can you identify your customer?"

The shopkeeper dreaded the reaction from Abinay, but he very slowly nodded in a negative. But this time, it was Lance who lost his cool. He pulled out his pistol from the back of his trousers and pointed it on the shopkeeper's head.

"Don't you dare lie! Do you understand? You are telling us a customer asked you to make the product, paid heavily for it and you cannot identify that person. And you think we will believe you, are you kidding me? Speak up the truth or trust me you will not live to see another sunrise!"

The shopkeeper shuddered as the cold metal touched his sweating temple. Abinay placed his palm on Lance's shoulder, signalling him to calm down.

"Hold your horses Lance, you need not use force all the time!"

Once again in the element of his calm, Abinay spoke, "Listen, you don't have to be scared if you have done no wrong. If you are innocent, no one will harm you. But you know what, this friend of mine seldom listens to me. Once he loses his mind, he cannot be tamed. So, my advice to you is to gently co-operate with us and tell us whatever you know. Otherwise he shall make you really uncomfortable!"

The shopkeeper felt his sight go blurred because of the fear Abinay had instilled in him even without touching him. He knew Abinay was not making up what he said. The shopkeeper whispered, "Officer, please trust me when I tell you that the man did not meet me in person. He contacted me on call and asked me if I could make a toy gun that could fire over six metres. The money was transferred to me on my mobile wallet. I was asked to deliver the toy near a dumping zone. I never had a chance to meet him in person. Please believe my word."

The fear he saw in the shopkeeper's eyes told Abinay that he wasn't lying. With a reassuring pat on the shoulder, he rose to his feet and pacing a couple of steps he spoke, "Is there anything you could tell us about your customer that could lead us to him. Anything?"

The shopkeeper thought for a couple of minutes, which seemed like eternity to an angry Lance. He stared at the shopkeeper; his eyes seemed to have turned amber in colour like live burning coal!

"Don't you hear what the man is asking? Tell him what he wants to know!"

The shopkeeper mustered all his courage and found enough voice to put together a trembling whisper, “Sir, when I went to drop the toy, I hid myself behind a tree to find out who my customer indeed was. I could not see his face as he had covered it with a joker’s mask and put on a hooded jacket. All I could notice was a strange design on the back of the jacket he was wearing.”

“Design?”

The deep lines on Abinay’s forehead had returned.

“What about the design?”

Abinay’s voice too lowered in excitement but was reassuring enough to make the shopkeeper feel he was being trusted. He continued, “I too deal in fancy clothing sometimes in my business, but I have never seen such a design on a jacket or T-shirt. It was unique, it was an image of a circle with nine spokes and a face of a lion in the centre.”

For a moment, Lance suspected the shopkeeper’s statement. A thought crossed his mind that the shopkeeper was very cleverly making up a story, as the description of the engraved arrow found in the hotel suite was leaked by the media. He was about to confront the shopkeeper once again, when Abinay stopped him. Both men left the shop and got on their way back to the headquarters.

But not before warning the shopkeeper to keep everything that they discussed strictly within the four walls of his shop. He was also asked for another piece of the same toy.

“Chief, why did you let him free? He was just making up a story, the description of the engraved arrow was leaked in the media. He could be very cleverly manipulating us. He is our prime suspect. And why do we need another sample of the toy?"

"You could be right Lance, but I don't want to leave any stone unturned. So, go find out if there is any fabric in the market with a matching design. Meanwhile I shall revisit whatever evidences we have found so far. Also, once the toy is in your custody, test its range of firing. Get to work Lance, we have no time to waste whatsoever!"

▼

As Abinay was reviewing all the evidences they had recovered already, he realized that the only mention of anything relatable thing to the engraved image on the arrow and the one described by the shopkeeper was the eight-spoke circle that Anvesha had talked about. Though this image had nine spokes in its circle.

He looked up on the internet about her and found multiple links line up on his monitor. One of them was of the recent TEDx talk in the city. After a couple of seconds of buffering, the video began playing. Five minutes into Anvesha's speech in the video, Abinay observed something that shook him.

He rewinded the video and paused it to see a man wearing a similar jacket as described by the shopkeeper, walk out of the auditorium. He had very cleverly made sure his face wasn't captured in the camera. Abinay re-examined the CCTV footage recovered from the hotel in which Yuyutsu died from two hours before Yuyutsu's death.

He could see Yuyutsu in the footage recovered from the reception camera, but did not find anyone in the jacket that was seen in Anvesha's TEDx talk video. Thinking where his next lead would come from, Abinay called Lance to find out if he was able to get some information on the jacket. He did not get response but a minute later, Lance entered the cabin.

"Chief, the design on the jacket the rogue shopkeeper described doesn't exist. My informers have confirmed to me that this design is nowhere in the market."

"Relax Lance! Your information is wrong. I know for a fact that the design on the jacket exists. See it for yourself."

"Chief, this is unbelievable! He could be our prime suspect and he actually has been captured on camera in the auditorium during the time that lady made her speech."

"Yes, but sadly that is all we have! He hasn't been captured in any of the hotel footages. If our hunch is right and the guy with the jacket is our culprit, he has very cleverly created an alibi for himself. Now we cannot use the shopkeeper's confession against anyone we see in the hotel footages. I tested the range of the toy he made for us and it fired close to fifteen feet."

Lance was still seated staring at the computer screen when his chief suddenly got to his feet and he was ordered to follow him out of the cabin to his car.

As both men neared the vehicle, Abinay signalled Lance to get into the driver's seat.

"Where to, Chief?"

"Cybercrime department!"

It was an hour-long silent drive, in which Lance chose not to disturb Abinay, who was lost in deep thought. The gate of the cybercrime campus opened automatically when Abinay swiped his identity card. Lance parked the car and both men walked into the building authorizing their credentials. Lance couldn't hold himself any longer.

"Chief, do you think these guys could access the scientist's hard disk?"

It only took a raised eyebrow from Abinay to silence Lance, who expected his superior to explode like a land mine. But Abinay responded very differently, "I hope they are able to, Lance, as this hard disk is the only chance we have to crack the mystery of Yuyutsu's death."

Moments later, they were amidst a group of techies stuck to their computers. Each screen ran endless rows and columns of zeros and ones. None of what he saw made any sense to Lance. The screens seemed to be talking to him in a language he did not understand. He blindly followed Abinay who walked straight into Manish's cabin where the cybercrime chief too was immersed in his computer screen and did not notice the two gentlemen enter his cabin.

"Manish, any progress on the hard disk recovered from the dead scientist's locker?"

"No officer, not yet! The encryption algorithm used in this case is quite complicated. This kind of encryption is not anything I have worked on ever before. Seems like something new, something very powerful."

"Can't you use brute force to crack the encryption?"

"No Abinay, brute force will not work in this case. The algorithm seems beyond brute force!"

Lance seemed all at sea. He wondered why couldn't brute force be used if all it takes to get the data out? He barged into the discussion, "Why are you guys contemplating so much to break this tiny thing? I can crush it to pieces with my bare hands!"

Lance casually moved towards Manish's computer to which the hard disk was connected. Abinay immediately held the man's wrist to stop him. The momentary strong hold on his wrist quickly made Lance understand that he was about to commit a grave mistake.

"Curiosity always kills the cat, Lance! Do not rush and do something you regret later. We need to be very careful at every step in our quest of solving this case."

Abinay spoke very calmly, but Lance knew his superior long enough to realize that firm resolve with which he was warned; he meant business. This strength of being calm in critical times and not putting down any of them, inspired them to go out of the way and do everything they could for the man they saw their leader in.

"Encryption and decryption of data is a very tricky business. In simple terms, encryption is like locking something and decryption obviously means an unlocking process with a pre-determined key.

"Use of brute force does not mean crushing the device and pulling its data out like some cops do with extreme criminals to get their confessions. Here, by brute force we don't mean using physical strength; brute force is the name of a computer encryption algorithm or methodology.

"This algorithm completely depends on sheer computing power to deduce and find out all the possible combinations of a potential key."

Both men were quite surprised to know Abinay knew about data encryption. But they were impressed, especially Manish.

"I am glad you understand the complexity involved in the task you have assigned me, Abinay. I guess you also might know about AES (Advanced Encryption Standard) or the Rijndael algorithm as it is popularly known. Cryptanalysts agree that AES is fool proof in all real-world applications. Though there are limited possibilities that this algorithm could be broken. However, these possibilities could be extremely rare.

"It is important to understand here that all global security agencies and anti-social organizations are forever competing with each other to stay a step ahead. I am afraid this time around we have fallen behind them. The algorithm that has been used to encrypt this hard disk is a very advanced version of the AES. Looks like someone has successfully build additional code to defend AES against the sideline attacks to the algorithm.

"Despite all our efforts, we might need some more time to unlock the disk. Meanwhile, I have already reached out to the global community of security agencies sharing the details we have gathered so far. If we get any help from across the globe, it might fast track the process. I don't intend to disappoint you, my friend, but for now, I have nothing else to tell you."

"I understand Manish, you need not explain. I know you always try your best. Keep me posted with any progress you make."

Abinay shook hands with him, acknowledged his efforts and started walking back towards their vehicle. Once again, Lance was struggling to hide his frustration.

"Chief, what do we do now? The hard disk was our window to unlocking all the secrets behind the scientist's death. Indeed, the secrets we uncover will lead us to his killer. Now with the window of opportunity blocked, how can we proceed further?"

Abinay gave a reassuring pat on Lance's back, "Don't worry boy, the thumb rule to success is to never quit. And in a job like ours, we often face hurdles. We must find alternative ways to achieve the desired goal, which are evidences. I am sure we will figure our way out."

The drive back to office was again a silent one and this time too, Abinay did not want to be disturbed. Till Lance broke the silence, "Chief!"

He cried impatiently, "I really believe we must learn more about the scientist, probably then we could find a way to unlock the hard disk. The best place to begin is ISA, the place he worked. Scientists usually are workaholic people, the maximum time of the day they spend is at work. Hence his colleagues are the people who would know him the best."

"You are right, Lance. Let us find out more about Yuyutsu. That will surely lead us to something meaningful. We shall visit the ISA first thing in the morning."

Lance nodded in agreement as it was almost end of working hours at the ISA and drove back to the headquarters. The rest of the day was eventless. But Abinay's mind was racing, thinking how he could find more about Yuyutsu, not just limiting himself to the information he would get from ISA.

Sometime in the middle of the night, he got up from his bed, walked up to his study, turned on his computer and launched the search engine. He typed,

Death of Yuyutsu Ghosh

All he could find were a handful of links that mentioned the dead scientist. Abinay was surprised not to see much online traffic for the information he sought. Not even ISA, for which Yuyutsu worked, had done much in mourning for one of its own. Apart from a condolence note on the official website, no employee had written anything on the official page, nor on social media.

Abinay found it very strange, knowing that in this modern age, people are so engrossed in social media that the number of likes their posts achieve becomes a matter of life and death. It is a great matter of status and a way of showing that everyone has an opinion. Yuyutsu's colleagues had not shown any purposeful reactions after his sad departure!

Such a cold response from one of the premier organizations in the country seemed very awkward to Abinay and he felt he had to investigate it. As this was on his agenda for the next morning, he decided to call it a night. But just before he was about to shut his computer down, he noticed the last link on the search results. It read,

In memory of my saviour….

The sentence seemed very emotional, though he hadn't yet read it completely. He clicked on it to take a closer look. The link navigated to a full blog page.

In fond memory of the man who was my saviour, the man who gave me the life I am living today! Yuyutsu Ghosh, an intellectual, a visionary and above all, a man with a golden heart!

Abinay didn't read the full write up, but he remembered the conversation he had with Yuyutsu's sister. She had mentioned that Yuyutsu had no family of his own. Then who was this person mourning for the dead man? Abinay had more questions than he had answers for. He immediately reached out to his mobile and scrolled down to the cyber-chief's number. As he was about to make the call, he held himself back. He did not want to bother him in the dead of the night, and decided to wait till next morning. But he himself twisted and turned all night in his bed.

The next morning, the first thing he did was to instruct Lance to go to ISA and find out as much as possible about Yuyutsu. He himself decided to go to the cybercrime department to check if they could fetch more information about the blogger who had written about the dead scientist. Lance was also very clearly instructed not to lose temper and create a scene in public.

In an hour, Abinay was in Manish's cabin telling him about the blog he had read the previous night. Manish read the blog himself and nodding in agreement said, "I know what you have to ask. You want me to trace the blogger from the information he or she would have registered on the blogging site. Isn't that what you expect?"

"Exactly! I believe this blog could answer a lot of questions we have about Yuyutsu and his death. That is why I need you to track down this blogger."

"That should not be a problem, all you need is an officially lodged complaint with an approval by the DGP. Then the blogging company will have to comply to the law of the land and provide the details of their registered customer. It should not take more than a couple of days."

▼

Lance sat in the ISA chief's cabin.

"An employee of your organization has been allegedly killed, and it doesn't seem to have made a difference to any of you."

The ISA chief reacted defensively, "That is not true at all, officer. It is indeed a loss to the science community!"

"If that is not true, why is it that there was no mourning organized by the organization?"

"We had, officer, but we do not believe in publicity. We in the science community believe the true service to mankind is by being totally committed and sincere to our profession. Yes, we mourned Yuyutsu's death, but we did not publicize our emotions towards him."

Lance rose to his feet and thudded his fists on the table that was between him and the ISA chief, at which the man across the table was taken aback.

"If I were to believe you sir, then why was Yuyutsu himself made to feel that he or his opinions were not valued in this organization? Otherwise why would an experienced scientist like Yuyutsu resign from the prestigious ISA after all these years?"

"What are you indicating, officer? Are you suspecting anyone of us involved in the death, or should I say the alleged murder of Yuyutsu Ghosh? If you are, officer, I would like to tell you that in the profession I am in and Yuyutsu himself was, discussions, disagreements and arguments are most likely to happen. Innovation is possible only through healthy discussions.

"As far as his resignation was concerned, he said it was a personal decision. I did ask him what he planned to do after resigning, but I did not get any answer."

"I agree sir, but what if any of those discussions were not as healthy as you think?"

In response, the elderly man exhaled deeply and trying to calm himself down, took a moment. He spoke with a pinch of bitterness in his voice, "Some years ago, an incident could have changed Yuyutsu's behaviour to a large extent. Something like that had never happened in the history of this prestigious organization. A great deal of miscommunication and confusion resulted in Yuyutsu being insulted. I guess Yuyutsu took the insult to heart and this changed him as a person. From that point of time, his relationships with colleagues and his attitude for the organization were never like before."

Narrowing his eyes, Lance questioned, "Then sir, could it be possible that one of those sour relationships resulted in Yuyutsu's death?"

The old man inhaled deeply, "Tell me something officer, do you like everyone you work alongside yourself and agree with everything they say? Would you kill them just because you don't like them?"

Lance sought for words to respond. It was time for the old man's turn to dart a disconcerting look or two at the police officer.

"I presume the answer is a no. Then how can you expect any other person to not have professional jealousy or politics torment him or her?"

The ISA chief could no longer hold his emotions and finally rasped aggressively.

"I am the one with the authority to question here, not you. I have nothing more to tell you officer, and I have more important things to attend to."

Lance was angry enough to get hold of the collar of the man in front of him and drag him to the police headquarters. But as instructed by Abinay, he wasn't supposed to do that. With an effort to hold on to his composure and to avoid a public burst out, Lance walked away, letting the ISA chief know he would return if he needed more information.

As Lance barged out and climbed on his classic Royal Enfield and was about to kick start it to roar its engine to life, his mobile vibrated. He was not surprised to see Abinay's number that had been saved as "Chief" flash on the mobile screen.

"Ycs chicf!"

He murmured trying to anticipate what new information Abinay could have gathered, but a long moment of silence poked him to realize he had called him to find out if he was able to fetch any details about Yuyutsu from the ISA. He did not know how to respond and after a second, he heard a penetrating voice from the other end, "Anything intriguing you found, Lance?"

There was still no response from Lance. When Abinay continued, "You need not fret, my friend. Come back to office. I need you for something important."

"I'll be there as soon as I can chief, but tell me what happened?" Lance asked anxiously.

Abinay responded in a crisp voice, "I have a lead on the blogger who had written about Yuyutsu. The cybercrime department has successfully traced the blogger and shared his details. We need to go and talk to him and gather all the information we need."

Soon, both men were driving through the busy traffic-stricken roads of the city. As bumpers kissed each other ever so slightly, both men realized that there was an ambulance stuck in the traffic right next to them. Though the traffic police constable struggled to clear the traffic, the situation was in no way coming under control. It seemed to be turning chaotic by the minute with every vehicle honking madly and the siren on the ambulance ringing desperately!

Lance lost patience after a while. He then got out of the car and rushed towards the traffic policeman. At that moment, Abinay thought his subordinate had lost his cool and was about to be harsh on the constable. To his pleasant surprise, he saw Lance at the helm of resolving the situation very calmly.

In a few minutes, the traffic started moving and Lance returned to the vehicle, to an appreciative pat on the shoulder from his role model. As they resumed the ride, Abinay's mobile phone vibrated. It was the control room calling him. Intrigued seeing the control room's number, he received the call, only to learn that his troubles with Yuyutsu's murder case had just seen a new twist.

Lance noticed the expression change on Abinay's face from an appreciative smile to an anxious one.

"What are you saying? Are you sure about it?"

The lines on his forehead dug deeper. Intrigued by the sudden change in Abinay's emotions, Lance asked, "What's wrong, chief? What happened?"

Abinay signalled with his hand to wait, Lance slowed the car and parked on the road side.

"Which hospital?"

"An ambulance just crossed us from the same hospital! Do you know the vehicle number? …Alright, send me the address of Manas Parthasarthi."

Abinay sighed deeply, caressing his forehead in what Lance would call disappointment rather than frustration. He wondered comparing himself to Abinay's calm demeanour, as he had figured out from the one-sided conversation that the vehicle number that was being asked for hadn't been noted. He himself would have by now roared like an angry lion in haste, if his subordinates hadn't worked as he expected. But Abinay maintained his poise.

Looking at Abinay, Lance understood that he had to follow the ambulance. For once, he thanked the slow moving traffic as the ambulance hadn't gone too far. As all the vehicles moved and the traffic got streamlined, Lance switched the siren on top of the police vehicle. Indicating that they were on route to something important and urgent, it helped them clear the way.

For a couple of kilometres the chase was on, the traffic added to Lance's irritation as he couldn't get ahead of the ambulance. Knowing Lance's mind like the back of his hand, Abinay did not need much time to understand that his subordinate had multiple questions popping in his mind. Abinay knew he had to quench the curiosity oozing in Lance's mind. "We have a new problem to deal with, Lance! There has been an attack on a neuroscientist Manas Parthasarthi and his cook. The neuroscientist is reported to have died by the time the ambulance reached for help. But the cook is barely holding on for dear life. He is being hospitalized as we speak."

"That is terrible, chief. But why are we being dragged into this case? We must deal with Yuyutsu's murderer. We cannot get distracted from this case, you must deny taking any new case. Is there no other officer in the department to handle?"

"You are mistaken, my friend. We were contacted because there is a huge commonality between the two cases."

"What do you mean, chief? What is the commonality between the two cases?"

There was anxiety and apprehension written all over Lance's face. There was a deafening silence in the car for a long moment. Abinay took a long pause before he finally spoke, "An exact same engraved arrow has been found in one of the house walls of the neuroscientist."

Lance felt his mouth go dry in shock and anticipation. He was short of words to say anything. He would have banged into a divider in the middle of the road, if he hadn't been warned by Abinay in time. Lance hit the brakes to bring the vehicle to a screeching halt. After a moment or two, when he had swallowed his sudden surge of emotions and brought himself some extent of self-control, he murmured, as he resumed to chase the ambulance, "Chief, this means both these cases could be deeply connected. Now it becomes imperative for us to get the culprit behind bars and solve this case that is fast entangling itself into an unresolvable knot. We must find the guilty and make sure he is brought to justice. Otherwise the city will panic. Already the psyche of people is heading in the wrong direction. If we don't mend the damage, the city will be in shambles."

"Chief, I also doubt that someone might have attempted to mislead us by using a similar arrow that we found as evidence in Yuyutsu's murder. The killer of Parthasarathi might have used the engraved arrow just to trick us, sending us on a wild goose chase!"

"That is for later, Lance. There is more to ponder about for now. This time around, a note has been left, along with the arrow."

"What kind of note? And why would anyone do that? If he has committed a grave crime like murder, that definitely could be a challenge in the form of a clue. You were right when you had said that Yuyutsu's killer is throwing an open challenge at us! But what was in the note?"

"The team wasn't able to figure that out. The note is blank. I will have to look at it myself, but first chase the ambulance. It might be taking the cook to the hospital. Hopefully we can get some information from him."

Lance wondered why would anyone leave a blank note? But did not want to add to the confusion, hence kept silence. He drove as fast as he could, making way wherever he could, honking as loudly as possible. After some distance, when the road was clear, the police SUV got adjacent to the ambulance and soon overtook it to block its way.

Without wasting a minute, Lance dashed out of the vehicle and knocked on the ambulance's driver window. The driver was shocked to see cops chasing the ambulance. He wondered in stunned silence what rule he had broken that the police came chasing him!

Lance signalled at him to lower the window, which he did instantly. He asked in a shaky voice, "What happened, sir? Did I overspeed or ignore any traffic rule? If I did, the only intention behind it was to save two innocent lives!"

"Who are you taking to the hospital?"

Lance rasped to the driver in a severe and cold tone, his voice shrinking the leftover courage in the driver. He felt Lance would smack him hard if he didn't respond in the next couple of seconds, the look in his eyes was so intimidating! He stammered his reply with great difficulty, "It's a pregnant woman, sir. She is whining in pain and needs medical attention as soon as possible. You can look for yourself."

In the next minute, Lance looked into the back entrance of the ambulance to find a whining and whimpering woman and her husband, who was trying to console her. Lance quickly got out and told the driver to continue his journey and returned to his vehicle. As Lance returned, Abinay was booking a cab to the dead neuroscientist Manas's address.

"Lance, you go get the blogger to the headquarters, meanwhile I shall go to Manas's residence. You join me there later."

▼

Abinay reached a small villa on the outskirts of the city. What seemed to be a deserted and lonely place on most days had turned into a hub of serious buzzing with the police and the media. The latter were prohibited entry to the crime scene.

Abinay barged his way into the gateway, wondering how the hell did the media always get to know. It irked him to no end when his own colleagues for couple of thousands of rupees leaked vital confidential information to the media. These journalists sensationalized the information shared to their benefit to generate higher TRP.

Abinay walked into the house, where a few constables were pacing in and out, trying to find some useful evidence. The first thing that stuck Abinay's watchful eyes was the arrow in the wall opposite to the door. But he chose to pick a pair of gloves and walked up to the dead body.

But he was relieved that no officer had touched the arrow, however he was sure the entire department was aware that he did not appreciate key evidence in his cases being manhandled without his approval.

He sat on his heals next to the dead body of Manas Parthasarthi. The body was clearly outlined with a chalk by the police officials who had reached at the crime scene in the first place. Besides the body was a dining table and chair and it was notable that the neuroscientist might have fallen off it.

On the edge of the table was a half empty glass of what looked like a home-based medicine. Manas was dressed in a T-shirt and a pajama. There was no mark of injury anywhere on the body. Abinay wondered, 'Does not look like a physical attack, then how did he fall? Could it be another curious case of poisoning using rare venoms? Did this guy too have convulsions like Yuyutsu? I hope the cook survives; he is the only eye-witness of his employer's death. This has to be a planned double murder case, otherwise why would anyone want to kill the cook?

'Obviously, whoever is responsible for Manas's death did not want him to have any chance of survival. That is why he removed every possibility of any help he could get. Or is it possible that the cook is creating an alibi by attacking himself? But first I need to see the arrow and the note tagged to it!'

Abinay got up to his feet, and with a pressing look on his face walked up to the wall where the arrow was stuck. He carefully plucked it out of the wall and noticed that it too was engraved like the one found at Yuyutsu's murder spot. But there was another thing tagged to the arrow, that aroused his curiosity more than ever. It was the small note hanging by the tail end of the arrow.

But as had been informed earlier, the note indeed was blank. He knew there had to be something more to the note. Abinay clinched his fist, the muscles around his neck notably swelled. His emotions about the killer clearly evident! Here was another taunting challenge thrown at him by the killer, as if he was telling him – *I am around the corner, catch me if you can!*

He called one of the constables and asked him to go and get a hair dryer, a couple of lemons, cotton buds and a paper cup. He added a bulb to the list, warning the constable to pay the shopkeeper and buy the dryer and not misuse his administrative power to get it. Meanwhile, he investigated the house for any evidence he could find.

He did not find anything curious anywhere, then he noticed two closed doors in the master bed room. As he opened one of them, he realized it was a bathroom. He wondered what could the other door lead to! As Abinay was about to open the second door and enter it, his mobile rang, flashing Lance's name on the screen.

"Chief!"

An enthusiastic voice spoke from the other end of the line, in a deep low voice he rasped, "Did you find the blogger Lance?"

The cold response from his superior told Lance that something had annoyed him. So, he humbly answered the question that was asked, "Yes Chief, I did. Actually, the boy identified the hard disk… that it belonged to his mentor and he was the one who encrypted the device. And he can unlock it!"

Abinay realized the reason of the excitement in his voice, and immediately softened his own voice, "That is brilliant! You have done a good job, my friend. Now leave the kid in the headquarters and quickly come here. We have a lot of work to do."

Abinay had just finished talking to Lance when the constable he had sent to buy the dryer and other items returned.

Abinay had to prioritize between the closed door in the master bedroom and the note tagged to the arrow that possibly had its content written in invisible ink. The choice was obvious, the latter. He clinically collected the lemon juice in the cup and began smearing it on the note with the cotton bud. While he let it dry on the piece of paper, he went back to the master bedroom to look what was in the other door.

As he twisted the knob, the door clicked open to total darkness as the room had no ventilation. He sprawled on the wall with his fingers to find the light switch. When he finally switched it on and there was light in the room, he saw a life size illusion paintings hung in the room. Intrigued to learn that the victim Manas was a painter too, Abinay walked towards the walls to take a closer look at the paintings. But just then, he heard a familiar voice, "Chief!"

"What took you so long Lance?

"Traffic!" Lance responded shrugging his shoulders meekly.

Abinay gave him a stare. "Send the dead body for postmortem and then examine this room closely. These illusionary paintings are bothering me, somewhat. By then, I'll figure out the curious note."

The lemon juice-smeared note was almost dry by now, but Abinay used the hair dryer to do the rest and then switched on the bulb. Holding the bulb in one hand and the note in the other just above the bulb, he saw the parts of the paper that were smeared with the juice turn brown and he was able to identify text that slowly became legible. The message read:

A wicked wife, a false friend, a saucy servant and a house with a serpent in it are nothing but death.

The quote seemed familiar to Abinay. He felt he had read it somewhere. But wasn't very sure about it. Walking a few paces, he tried to recall the speaker who had quoted the line in the note. While he was trying dig up his mind to remember something about the quote, Lance came rushing from the room Abinay had asked him to examine.

"Chief!"

There was a notable alarm in his voice, which broke the chain of thoughts in Abinay's mind. He turned to look at an impatient Lance, "What is it, Lance?"

Abinay asked, seemingly flustered for a change. Guessing his mood, Lance decided to listen to what was bothering his senior officer rather than blurting out his own concern.

"You tell me chief, you look perturbed. Can I help?"

"It's this quote Lance. I have read it and I am very familiar with it. But I am not able to recall who said it. I feel the quote could lead us to clues in this case."

"What does the quote say, chief?"

Abinay handed the processed piece of paper to the probing Lance, who wanted to know how the paper had changed colour from white to a tinge of brown, to which Abinay reiterated the entire procedure that he had clinically carried out to decipher the invisible quote.

"That must be a powerful and super secretive message in that note, chief! Otherwise why would anyone write in invisible ink? The plot of these murders is thickening… seems like the conspiracy of the Mauryan times."

Abinay turned sharply to face Lance, a sudden relief in his face. Lance did not understand the sudden change of emotion.

"Thanks Lance, you answered the question flip-flopping in my head. This quote of course was spoken by Chanakya, the chief advisor of Chandragupta Maurya! But what is it pointing to? Why has the killer tagged it along the arrow?"

Lance had relieved Abinay from the question on the speaker of the quote, but had also had brought new concerns. He felt shifting his focus for a while would give him some much-needed time to think of new perspectives and possibilities.

"Let it be Lance, you sounded quite alarmed when you came from inside. What did you see in that room?"

"Yes chief, what that room leads to is shocking. Come with me at once, you have to see it!"

Curious enough, Abinay followed Lance into the attached door in the master bedroom. As the men stepped inside the room, they saw walls covered with four life-size illusion paintings. One was an all-watching eye, the other was a man pointing his finger at the audience. The third painting was of a woman with a finger on her lips, and each one of the paintings seemed as real as it can get, but Lance brought Abinay's focus to one painting, that was of seven doors opening one behind the other.

"Chief, feel this painting."

Abinay knotted his eyebrows; he was a little confused, but he touched the painting. To his surprise, he realized that the material he felt wasn't a canvas or anything on which usually art work is done. It was wood using which the doors were carved. Taking cue from Lance's nod, he pushed the door-like painting, and it opened to a long series of stairs leading into a dungeon.

"Did you follow the steps into the dungeon?"

"I thought it was better you saw it first."

Lance led the way with his mobile torch on, followed by Abinay with his pistol and a couple of constables. The long stretch of steps led to a totally dark tunnel-like structure, that ended in a starlit large space. It looked like an advanced laboratory with hi-tech equipments all over the place and a couple of them were half-made too. There were a bunch of super computers and a couple of huge speakers connected to the super computers.

But the flooring below their feet wasn't too fancy, as it was of cow dung. The men wondered why the neuroscientist had this weird set up underground, if it was only a research lab?

"There has to be more to this place…"

Abinay rasped in a low voice, clinching his jaws!

"Lance, do you have network in your phone? I don't."

"No chief, even I don't, probably because we are several feet underground."

"Alright, let's go back to the house and find out the condition of the cook. I hope he gets better. I think we won't find anything more till we open the safe."

Abinay said folding his arms on his chest and exhaling deeply. By now he knew the computer would be well encrypted and he would need Manish again. As the three men began walking back, the constable noticed some difference in the floor below.

"Sir, you might want to come here and take a look at this."

"What is it?"

Both Abinay and Lance rushed to where the constable was pointing to, he was feeling the piece of land.

"Sir, these beetles! These are usually found in burial grounds, they feed on decomposing human corpses."

"There is only one way to know then. That could be a vital observation. Get tools to dig the place!"

Lance returned to the house to find out about the cook's health, while the constable came looking for some tools to dig up the dungeon area. Abinay decided to stay in the lab.

As the constable got the tools to dig up the floor, Lance walked with a dull face.

"What's wrong with you?" Abinay asked with a knowing look on his face. As if he expected what was coming.

"The cook did not survive…" Lance uttered in a disappointed tone. Abinay exhaled deeply, his hands on his waist. He realised he had been pushed back to square one. He had hinged his hopes of learning more about Manas's killer from the cook. But now he had to find new ways to get to the guilty. He had learnt from experience, there was no perfect crime and there would be clues left over. It was up to him to find them.

On the other hand, the two constables were digging away the floor, until they made an unsettling revelation, a human skeleton! Lance stepped closer to see if he could find anything else.

"Chief, who could this be now? The state of the corpse tells us it has been here for quite some time and has been well guarded too. I'll send the bones to the forensics and the electronic equipment to the cybercrime team at once."

Abinay nodded and started walking up the steps that had brought him down there, as if he knew there was nothing more the dungeon would fetch him. As the police team cordoned off the entire site, the two men who mattered started towards the headquarters.

▼

Abinay was back in his office, sitting on his cushiony chair with his right leg on his left knee and his right elbow resting on the chair's arm, twisting one end of his mush upwards.

"Rahul, right? How do you happen to know the dead scientist? I hear you hold him at quite a high pedestal in life!"

"Yes sir, Yuyutsu Ghosh was my godfather. I owe every breath of mine to him. My life is his charity sir! I grew up in an orphanage with the charity he did."

Abinay rose to his feet and walked behind Rahul and patted his hands on the young man's shoulders. As he paced around looking outside the window of his office, he continued, "What do you do Rahul? As in for a living..."

"I am a college drop out by choice sir, so I don't have a proper job. But I earn my bread by doing ethical hacking."

"So, you are a computer genius? Is that the reason why you said you can unlock the hard disk?"

"No sir, I had encrypted the hard disk, that's why I can decrypt it."

"What! You encrypted it?"

Lance jumped to his feet!

"Then do you know what is in it?"

Lance's eyes hooked on to Rahul as he bent over on the arms of the chair the boy was sitting on. For a second, Rahul was stunned to silence.

Abinay turned around to face Rahul, "Don't scare the kid Lance, he is innocent. Listen Rahul, as you said Yuyutsu could be a very good man. But he has allegedly been murdered. We need the data in that hard disk to find the killer. Can you help us?"

Rahul took a moment to process all that Abinay had just said and digest it. Then he slowly nodded his head in an affirmative. "Yuyutsu sir was indeed a great man! I never asked him any question when he told me to do something. That is why I did not ask him anything about the data in the disk. I just encrypted it. If it helps you find his killer, I will help you."

Abinay signalled Lance to take the boy to the cybercrime department, as a constable requested to step in.

"Sir, there is a visitor to see you. She says you asked her to come."

"Is it Anvesha Roy? Yes, I had asked her to come, let her in immediately."

Anvesha entered the cabin, looking as ravishing as anyone could. For a moment Abinay felt a cool breeze grace his face as she stepped in. But the next moment, he had regained absolute focus on things at hand.

"Please have a seat, ma'am. I really appreciate you honouring my request and coming over."

"No problem officer, tell me how I can be of any help? Is this regarding the twin murder case of the neuroscientist and his cook that was reported a little while ago in the news?"

Abinay rose to his feet, switched the projector on and flashed the image of the arrow recovered at Manas Parthasarthi's residence. Anvesha narrowed her eyes looking at the image. With confusion written all over her face, she asked, "Why are you showing me the arrow recovered in Yuyutsu's murder scene? What does it have to do in this case?"

"They look the same ma'am, but they are two different arrows. They aren't the only reason I had to reach out to you."

He pointed to the next image that had flashed on the screen, it was the note tagged to the arrow with the strange quote. Anvesha not only identified the quote but also noticed the golden-brown patches all over the piece of paper. Blinking at Abinay with intrigue in her eyes, "This is a quote by..."

"Chanakya!" Abinay completed Anvesha's sentence.

"I assume the golden-brown marks on the paper are because the words were invisible, and you treated it with heat to make the words visible. You now think that the theory I proposed last time in Yuyutsu's murder, of the ancient secret society has set itself in action!"

"Not me, but someone might be, more so because I suspect poisoning the reason for the death of the neuroscientist. The postmortem report is yet to confirm it, though."

"I know where you are coming from, officer. Poison was a popular method used for assassinations in ancient India. Alexander the great died after suffering greatly for twelve days. There is a possibility that he might have died of drinking wine made of a toxic plant that looked innocuous to the eye, but when fermented turns deadly poisonous. There are many such plants and animals that have been identified as toxic."

Anvesha noticed that Abinay seemed a little confused, she paused, "Is there something that you don't agree with officer?"

"Doesn't history claim that Alexander died of malaria or typhoid? Didn't he?"

Anvesha smiled shaking her head in a firm negative. "Officer, you have heard what has been propagated as the four most popular theories about Alexander's death. Three of which can be discounted, let me explain to you. Malaria is carried by mosquitoes that live in jungles and tropical regions. But not near deserts of central Iraq where he died. Typhoid is transmitted by food and water infected by the bacteria; there is no historical data to suggest there was such an outbreak around the time he died.

"The third theory of alcohol poisoning can also be discounted because the main effect of alcohol poisoning is continual vomiting, but there is no mention of any vomiting or even nausea in any records related to the leader's death. That leaves the last theory that looks most probable, that of a toxic substance that pervaded in his body and very slowly took effect.

"But the question that stupefies most historians or anyone who follows the mystery of Alexander's death is that if he was poisoned, what kind of poison was administered to him? Because though he was subject to unbearable agony, the toxin did not kill him quickly.

"Toxins like arsenic, strychnine would have killed him almost instantly. The same applies to poisons like wormwood, hemlock and many more. It is a fact that Alexander lived for twelve long agonizing days, giving solid reason to not consider them as toxic agents that killed him.

"However, research and literature to support it clearly show that there are plants like white hellebore, a white flowering plant that can be fermented into poisonous wine. The symptoms of consuming this plant perfectly fit with the description of what Alexander experienced for over twelve days before death.

"Now coming to our original discussion, that is poison being used in ancient India to shift power forcefully from one hand to another. Yes, it is true that poison was used as a popular method of assassinations. This could be a very strong connection between the assassinations in ancient times and these killings.

"Not only because you suspect Manas has been poisoned like Yuyutsu. Or because you found the note with Chanakya's quote, but also because of the kind of expertise Chanakya possessed over toxicology. Legend says that because poisoning was very popular tool used for assassinations to change regimes, Chanakya began adding small amounts of poisons in Chandragupta's food to make him immune to every kind of venom over a period.

"But because everything in life has a flip side to it, the activity of adding poison to Chandragupta's food to develop his immunity against attacks too had a flip side!"

Anvesha exhaled deeply; to which Abinay planted another imposing question, "If that was an attempt to secure the king, how can it have any implications?"

"As Chandragupta Maurya's immunity against immunity grew stronger, Chanakya steadily increased the potency of the toxins in the king's food platter. That meant the toxicity of the amount of poison added could not be tolerated by most. Especially by those who were in a sensitive state of health conditions. The queen in her pregnancy was no exception, she had no knowledge of the exercise Chanakya and Chandragupta were carrying out. One morsel of the plate was enough to bring the king's world falling apart.

"Dhurdhara reached her deathbed in no time after eating that morsel from her husband's plate. Even Chanakya couldn't save her from the inevitable, but he managed to save the baby by cutting the queen's belly. A dark mark on the child's forehead was believed to be the effect of the poison that entered the baby.

"Actually officer, the fact of the matter is that developing immunity against poisons, that modern medical system calls antidote isn't limited to India. Archeologists have found that native Americans of the ancient civilizations considered poisoned arrows very lethal as they tested them against a number of medicines. This has been a legitimate weapon in ancient and modern times and has even been used in cold wars across the globe."

As Anvesha paused, Abinay moved his fingers in his hair, thinking how to join the dots of the information overload he was being showered with.

"All that is very interesting and intriguing to listen to for the contents of a page-turning novel. But could it be true that someone related to this two thousand-year-old secret society can be behind all this? The idea of such a possibility itself is unbelievable and stupefying. Is there anything more that you could tell me about the secret society that would seem more realistic and relatable?"

"Officer, as I had mentioned in my TED Talk, there is no credible or solid proof about the group's existence. This is true not only for this group, but most secret societies across the globe. But there are few things that have leaked through the centuries about 'The Unknown Nine'."

Narrowing his eyes Abinay asked curiously, "The group has a name?"

With a striking look in return, "Why not, officer? If the West could create globally popular secret societies like the Freemasons and name them based on the occupation of most members, why do you think an Indian secret society doesn't deserve a name? However, historians and mystery enthusiasts who believe in the existence of the group are of the opinion that the group was given the name for a reason. Unlike the groups in the West, this group has always been limited to nine members.

"As a believer in the existence of the society, my first argument would be a comparison with the *Mahabharata*. There is enough and more evidence like the remains of the divine city of Dwarka found in the ocean bed. Now if you talk about more recent times, there are references that you could make. A book on the 19th century French administrators like Louis Pauwels and Jacques Bergier, formed a solid base to the belief of the group's existence.

"There are conspiracy theories against all the secret societies that are believed to have existed at some point in time. That these organizations sought to all kinds of ways to enhance their hold over societies. Though their existence has never been confirmed, they have always secretly been expanding. This is the key difference between 'The Unknown Nine' and the rest of the secret groups, that they never tried to expand.

"One of the founding principles of this group was that it had to sustain itself within the chosen nine. From ages, the number nine is believed to be an auspicious number. There are a number of such examples across cultures, especially in Indian history. There are nine celestial influencers in Indian astronomy, nine universal elements in Hindu philosophy.

"Many rulers – be it Akbar, Krishnadevaraya, Vikramaditya or Chandragupta himself – had nine intellectuals in their court. The number has found special significance even in foreign cultures and rituals. For the Hebrews, it is the number of truth. Christianity believes, the ninth hour is the hour of prayer. In Chinese faith, the number nine is associated with the dragon, the symbol of magic and power."

"Are you saying that 'The Unknown Nine' never did anything unethical and if they ever existed, as you say they did, they were clean of any wrong doings?"

"As long as 'The Unknown Nine' would have lived by the rules Chanakya set for them, they could not have done anything unethical. He never made a mistake in identifying the character or personality of anyone. He never chose the wrong person for the job. If that was the case, the Mauryan Empire could never have flourished the way it did.

"Coming back to the details of the society, there have always been powerful leaders all along the history of India who have had their say in how the country and society is governed. Chanakya was definitely one of them. He was not only a master advisor and shrewd politician, but a great visionary, intellectual and an enlightened mind himself.

"In his times, Universities of Taxila and Nalanda attracted students from across the globe, as they were great learning centres. Perhaps great scholars were there who recorded all the scientific enhancements of that time. May be inspired from them, he advised the king to create the secret society."

"In such a scenario, ma'am, the descendants or successors of those chosen nine might be anywhere in the world?"

"For sure officer! In fact some historians believe that Chanakya had gathered the nine masters before Ashoka became the undisputed king of the subcontinent. But after the carnage in the Kalinga battle, he brought the nine men in contact with Ashoka.

"Chanakya then convinced the king to send these masters to distant lands in the guise of Buddhist monks to spread the message of peace and non-violence. Hence, not allowing all the power of knowledge to concentrate in one place. They were also advised to continue their research. In order to keep the knowledge growing and flourishing, so that it could be put to the right use of betterment of humanity.

"Most people in this modern era are pseudo-intellects who do not believe in the reality of *Mahabharata*, but Chanakya did and that is why he followed what was the tried and tested method of knowledge transfer. It is believed that after the great war of Kurukshetra, between the Kauravas and Pandavas, Krishna advised king Yudishthira, the eldest Pandava to go to Bheeshma, who had immense knowledge of centuries and decentralize it.

"This theory, officer, goes fairly well with the logic that after the decline of the Mauryan Empire, the scientific and sociological advancement dipped drastically."

"Bygones are bygones, ma'am. Even if all this is true, these are centuries old and obsolete. Is there nothing you could tell me that is more recent, anything that occurred at least in the 1990s if not the 2000s?"

Anvesha nodded with a smile, sarcasm written all over her face, "I knew you would ask me this question officer. Yes, I can tell you about a few incidents from the twentieth century. Believers in their existence, including me, argue that whenever the time was right, the nine provided the required help in scientific advances in India.

"In the 1980s, India was looking to develop massive GSLV rockets capable of launching satellites into the 24-hour orbit, that could carry Indian astronauts to the moon. Back then, India was the only country amongst the developing nations which had the potential to reach space at an ultra-low cost. This would have put top space agencies out of business.

"Conspiracy theorists believe that top international agencies came together to conspire against India and its aggressive space ambitions. At least hold our space program back as long as possible, that was why international pressure was built on Russia and they didn't provide us the cryogenic engines that were the heart of a GSLV rocket. Indian scientists were denied of the technical support they needed.

"There are conspiracy theories that 'The Unknown Nine' assisted the Indian space scientists to develop the needed technology indigenously. Opposers might question, if the secret society helped the space agency, then why couldn't they fast track the development of the technology? Why did it need two decades?

"What they fail to understand was that no scientific innovation can happen overnight in discouraging environments. India for a very long time did not enjoy the environment in which science and technology could thrive!"

By the moment Anvesha completed her sentence, her voice reeked of angry and disappointed vibes. Abinay was about to say something to comfort her, when his mobile screen flashed Lance's name.

"What is it that you have found that you want me to come immediately to the cyber department?"

"Chief, it's better you come and see for yourself!"

"Ma'am, I'll have to take your leave now, but I will need your assistance once the postmortem report confirms the cause of Manas's and his cook's death. Also, I want to warn you about something very important. In the course of our investigation, we found evidence in your recently concluded TEDx talk... Probably you too are being watched closely."

Anvesha was stunned to silence. She couldn't fathom the possibility of her being watched and followed. She swallowed her surprise and uttered, "Why would anyone keep a watch on me? And what evidence did you find during my talk that you found intriguing?"

There was a sense of anxiety in that question from the lady, as if she felt she was a suspect. Abinay noticed it and said, "No offense ma'am, I am not suspecting you, but yes the evidence we found seems to be a key one. A person was caught on video wearing a jacket with the same image as found on the arrow head. Hence, I think if the killer is one of the believers in 'The Unknown Nine' like yourself, he might be watching you. That is why I want you to be careful, because we cannot be sure of his next move."

▼

Soon Abinay was sitting in Manish's cabin in the cybercrime office. Lance too was there along with the young blogger, Rahul.

"Abinay, Rahul helped us unlock the hard disk, it was a very smartly written algorithm. But what we found is beyond us to comprehend."

"Really? What have you found that is so complicated? Let me have a look."

Manish opened a folder in which there were files with strange looking single character file names.

"Did you see that chief? I don't understand what this scientist was trying to hide so effectively. This looks like some alien language to me. He seriously must be a laughing stalk in his community. No wonder he was ridiculed. Maybe he tried to pull off some stupidity in the space agency and was accused of theft of intellectual property."

"Wait a minute Lance, this isn't an alien language. I can identify these characters. These are numbers in ancient Sanskrit. But the question you are posing is valid. Why would a space scientist like Yuyutsu own something like this, more so hide so securely, content written in an ancient language?"

'Did I have less puzzles in my plate already, that I was brought a new one?' Abinay clinched his jaws in frustration, but the next moment he calmed himself to seem normal, as if everything was in his control. He looked around to see if the people around him had noticed his momentary loss of composure! He knew that this wasn't the time to lose temper.

"Manish, are these the only things you found on the disk?"

"No Abinay, this isn't all. There is more that we have… it is one folder that has random text file and .exe file in a folder. I ran the .exe with the text file as an input and it generated blank image as output of which we couldn't make any sense. No message was found in the image.

"Rahul too doesn't have any clue about it. He says it might have been encrypted before he was asked to encrypt the disk and he did not look into the contents of the disk."

"No message too is a kind of message, isn't it?"

"You are right Abinay, it is an ancient encryption method in which messages could be concealed in different media, and images are one such medium. The image needs a key for the concealed message to be extracted. But that isn't all, this image file is encrypted using a very intelligent algorithm! If you fail to unlock it in the first attempt, it will not give you a second chance. As it is a self-destructing file. We need to be very careful or we will lose the secret it beholds forever."

Abinay thought for a moment, "Get me the images of the evidences that we collected in Manas Paarthasarthi's house, Lance."

In the next ten minutes, Lance had all the images in his phone. He seemed confused about which image his chief wanted to look at. Unable to decide, he gave Abinay his phone so that the man could look at whatever he needed to. Scrolling through the pictures, he stopped at the images of the illusion paintings found in Manas's house.

"Don't look so confused guys, it is evident that both murders are related. The link between both killings has to be related to this secret." Abinay knew the encrypted file was like a ticking bomb. If anything went wrong, the investigation could hit a dead end.

"This is one single eye, in this the next picture there is one pointing finger. In the next painting there are two lips and one finger. But here the focus is on keeping silent, so we must focus on one speaking mouth. Lastly the five doors are obvious, aren't they? The key probably could be 1115. Only one way to find out, though! Let me key in the numbers."

All the men in the room crossed their fingers. The theory Abinay had deduced seemed logical. But it was a risk none the less, and had to be taken.

As he double clicked on the image file, an input box popped up on the screen with an OK button that was disabled. As he keyed in the four numbers, the OK button got enabled, but just before submitting the key, he stopped.

"Wait a minute! The finger pointing in the painting is one, but in the background, there are actually five. This could be a trick to fail any attempt of cracking the encryption, I am changing the entry to 1515. Also, Manish, can you record everything that happens on this system?"

"Yes, I can, I just have to run a simple script, but why do you want to record?"

"As you said, this file destroys itself after one attempt of decrypting it. It could also be possible that it might get destructed even if we decrypt it successfully. You never know!"

The system took a moment to respond, which seemed too long to everyone present. Everyone held their breath, hoping the file didn't destroy itself and cause the loss of the secret. A moment later the screen flashed another text file, that read a bunch of junk characters,

"CEDBEAECBCEAEABDBAEDAEABADCBCBDBAA"

"1213134513452323433112"

In few seconds, it closed and deleted itself. Exactly as Abinay had expected.

"Good lord Abinay, we could have lost the file if we hadn't recorded every activity as per your instructions."

"Alright, I also want you to send the rest of the data to me. I will study it. Meanwhile, let me call Dr Pashupathi to check on the postmortem report of Manas and his cook."

He pulled out his phone and was about to make the call when he saw the doctor's name flash on the phone screen.

"Doctor, what a pleasant surprise! I was about to call you. Was wondering if you found something on the corpses of the neuroscientist and his cook."

"I thought as much officer, otherwise why would you remember me, right?"

"Well sir, that is my job. I am looking forward to hear from you."

"Yes, I have loads to tell you. Come over to my office."

▼

Dr Pashupathi and Abinay were soon sitting opposite to each other in his office. As he sipped his typical strong filter coffee, he spoke, "I have completed the postmortem of two of the three deceased. Both Manas and his cook have died of acute pulmonary edema, which means…"

"Doctor, I know what pulmonary edema means, it is a condition in which lungs fill with fluid. In such a condition the body struggles to get enough oxygen and the victim experiences shortness of breath. In the simplest of words, it is also known as lung congestion, am I right?"

"Indeed, you are officer! You have learnt on your job; unlike many in your department. That is why I like working with you."

Dr Pashupathi genuinely appreciated Abinay's work ethics. The feeling was mutual between the two men. The appreciative smile was soon replaced by a familiar curious look in one and all knowing confidence in the other.

"Go ahead officer, clarify your doubt that is waiting to be fired in your head. I know what it is anyway."

"The circumstantial evidence very strongly indicates that both Manas and his cook were murdered. I also suspect some kind of poison could be the cause of their death. But you are saying that they died of lung congestion. Do you mean that my suspicions are baseless?"

"Officer, I said that both victims died of lung congestion, true; that need not mean it couldn't be the result of any poison, does it?"

Dr Pashupathi winked at Abinay, patting his back.

"Your suspicion is right, my friend. The lung congestion is definitely the result of a deadly poison indeed. Not only that, my extensive experience of decades has taught me enough to figure it out when I am dealing with linked homicides. I suspect that the murders of both Yuyutsu and Manas could be linked."

"Yes doctor, my investigation too indicates something similar. But why do *you* think so?"

"Alright officer, let's understand the reason I said that. If you recall, the cause of Yuyutsu's death was…"

Abinay cut Pashupathi in between, "I remember every word of your report, doctor. Yuyutsu was killed by a very rare venom of South American wild frogs. That is called Batrachotoxin and is extremely potent in nature."

"Exactly, officer; Batrachotoxin is indeed a very potent poison. Now coming to Manas and his cook's death, I have completed my forensic investigation. The findings blew my mind. I haven't seen anything like this in my career. Two homicide cases with venoms that are extremely rare and very potent. But of very different sources."

"What are you saying, doctor? Could you please elaborate?"

Sipping the last few drops of his filter coffee, Dr Pashupathi rose to his feet. With great difficulty, he carried his overflowing belly weight on his feet, deeply exhaled and spoke, "Our culprit here seems to be an expert toxicologist. He is using potent poisons on his targets, making sure his victims have no chance of survival. Only difference is that this time he has chosen to use a poison from a very common but lethal source."

"What is it now? Don't tell me it's a poison made of pumpkin seeds!"

"You are half right officer, it is indeed a deadly poison from a plant source. But is not from pumpkin seeds. Ricin on the other hand is a product, naturally available in castor plant, commonly known as castor beans. Despite not being technically a bean. The castor plant is extremely common, as it can grow anywhere."

"Are you kidding me doctor? Castor oil is something we have in all our homes. In our childhood we were even made to drink it to cleanse our digestive systems. How can it be poisonous?"

"I said castor beans are poisonous, not castor oil. Ricin is not present in the oil, but it is a protein left behind in the mash of the castor beans. In fact, it is not difficult to make."

"You mean a poison can be extracted at home even by common people?"

"Again, you are half right officer. Ricin extraction is not rocket science. But trying to do so without the right precautions and knowledge could be like signing your own death note! That is the reason I said the killer of both Yuyutsu and Manas is an expert toxicologist.

"To answer your question though, yes. Ricin can be extracted using a process called Chromatography, a process of separating mixtures by dissolving a suitable solvent or gas."

"Doctor, if pulmonary edema was the cause of both the deaths, it is most likely that they would have inhaled the poison. In that case, the amount poison that killed both Manas and his cook could be very less."

"Yes Abinay, the cause of the lung congestion is definitely inhalation of Ricin. Because the symptoms of ingestion of the poison are very different. Ingestion would have caused gastrointestinal effects like severe vomiting and diarrhea, leading to acute dehydration. Then the Ricin infects the cells of gastrointestinal organs as it flows through the body, leading to the failure of kidneys, lever and pancreas.

"On the other hand, injection of the toxin causes different reactions depending on where the victim has been injected. But generally, it results in flu-like symptoms, inflammation of the injected area, and eventually, organ failure. But inhalation as in this case results in bloody cough, lung congestion, difficulty in breathing and finally death.

"Ricin is a kind of poison that is deadly in any way it enters your system. In case of both inhalation and injection, death is almost certain after 4 to 5 miserable and agonizing days. Also, if inhaled, as in this case, it only requires 1.78 milligrams of the toxin to kill an adult. That is equal to a few grains of table salt, which ricin resembles visually.

"My forensic investigation also indicates a very strong infection in both victims, that was 4 to 5 days old.

"The protein in Ricin infects cells, blocking their ability to synthesize its own protein. Without the cells making their protein, the vital organs of the body and their functionality cease eventually, causing death. Even survivors suffer permanent organ damage. Scientist across the globe are trying to find an antidote to this toxin, hence the centre for disease control and prevention has bluntly stated on its website that no antidote exists for Ricin."

Dr Pashupathi poured himself another cup of filter coffee and offered some to Abinay, who declined it. His mind was stuck on another question, "Doctor, if Ricin is really as dangerous as you say, why hasn't it been used extensively in history? Have there been instances of Ricin being used in assassinations of world leaders?"

"Officer, there is no doubt in Ricin being a deadly poison, but its effectiveness is maximum when it is used as a bio-weapon in close contact. Compared to poisons like Anthrax, Sarin or Botulinum, Ricin's potency as a weapon of mass destruction becomes limited. Because the protein ages and becomes ineffective fairly quickly. In the background of the First World War, the US conducted several experiments to prepare wide scale Ricin weapons.

"Packaging Ricin into bombs and bullets did not prove effective. Hence the US government discarded them. But there have been assassinations using Ricin as a close contact weapon. In the year 1978, the Bulgarian secret service with the assistance of KGB, the secret service of the then USSR, killed a novelist, playwright, journalist and dissident Georgi Markov.

"In short, officer, the killer of Manas and Yuyutsu is making a loud statement. I can't think of any other reason why he is killing people with such intriguing methods. If you fail to figure out why is he doing this, then I am sure we are going to see hell break lose! This will have far-reaching repercussions. I only hope, you find the missing pieces of the puzzle together and end the killing spree."

"I'll do my best doctor, but as soon as you complete the forensics on the third body, let me know. My gut feel says the deceased has a key role in this case."

"Sure officer, upon first look the skeleton found seems to be in the stage five of decomposition. That explains the presence of beetles around it. But a deep dive would uncover more."

"I need one more favour from you doctor. Can you get me Manas's finger prints?"

"I know the body would have begun decomposing, but could you try? I made a mistake by not getting it for Yuyutsu's too before handing the body to the family. The way the data has been protected in this case, my gut feel says we might need biometrics of everyone involved."

"You are right officer, it is a tricky process to recover fingerprints after a person is dead. Because biometrics is all about body measurements, in computer circles these body measurements are used to identify a person. After a person dies, his or her body starts decomposing, as early as four hours after the time of death. This results in the body shrinking and tightening.

"I am sure you know that this biological decomposition is called Rigor Mortis. As a result of which body measurements change and that is why biometrics becomes difficult. Most modern biometric systems use a capacitive touch approach. That means they use the electric signals generated by the human skin to build a highly specific digital map of the ridges and valleys of the human fingers. After death, it is difficult to reproduce an exact print pattern of the finger. But it is still possible, using the simple dental mold models along with conductive silicon or gelatin. I think I can pull it off."

"That will be of great help, doctor. I cannot thank you enough."

"You do your job officer, I will do mine. Good luck!"

▼

The next day, Abinay did not go to the headquarters, instead he asked Lance to meet him at his residence.

"Is all well, chief? Why did you ask me to come here? I was planning to go to the second crime scene, Manas Parthasarthi's residence."

"Yes, all ok. I asked you to come here because we need to see my father in my village. He is the only one who I think can guide us further in this case. Send some other officer to collect the sample evidence from the crime scene."

Lance nodded as Abinay instructed, "Meanwhile, ask some of our officers to check if there was an air-conditioner installed in Manas's house. If yes, it has to be tested for the presence of Ricin particles. Manas and his cook died due to lung congestion. The AC might be the root cause. Also ask the officers who are securing the crime scene to watch out for the jacket man. I have a hunch he might show up."

Abinay's father was a high school teacher in the village's government school. It did not make sense when Lance was told that the old school teacher was the only one who could lead them further in this intriguing and twisted triple murder case.

Looking at his puzzled subordinate's face, Abinay figured out what might be troubling him.

"My father is not only a retired school teacher, but one of the few Vedic astronomers left in the country. As I told you, the content of the hard disk is in chaste Sanskrit. When I was scrolling through the files, I found a design of some kind of a hi-tech equipment too. If my father could read the text, we might get some clue about the equipment and lead us further in our investigation."

In a couple of hours, Abinay and Lance were in front of Abinay's father's house. Recognizing the vehicle number, the old man was happy. But also surprised to see his son visit him without prior information, that too on a working day. The old man hurried to the gate. "Son, is all well? What brings you home so suddenly? That too in the middle of a busy week. Why are you here instead of working towards solving the recent famous murder mystery in your city?"

"Don't worry dad, I am working on a case and that is what has brought me here, seeking your help."

Lance was astonished at the professional conversation the father and son duo were having. He had expected a warm greeting, but saw none.

"What are you saying, Abinay? Your investigation brought you to my doorstep, that is intriguing."

Lance was still lost in the conversation both father and son had just had. Abinay looked at him and asked what was he thinking.

"Chief, you and your father always have such conversations?"

"Of course not, Lance. But my father expects me to be a good cop, even if I don't prove myself as a worthy son! Come on in, my friend! Now you shall see my dad behave as if I am only a cop and not his son."

"Tell me officer, how can I be of help in your investigation? I'll do all that is in my capacity as a responsible citizen."

"Sure sir, but before that, meet my colleague, officer Lance. Officer Lance, meet my father, Narsimha Chaturvedi."

Lance extended his arm in a hand shake, to which the old man responded in a humble namaste and a welcome smile.

Once the men were for the house, Abinay opened the folders and files he had received from the cybercrime department.

"Sir, here is some content I would like you to go through and translate it for us. I believe your guidance will lead us further."

The old man put on his spectacles and took a closer look at the text, then after a few minutes, spoke with a spark of excitement in his voice.

"This text is from the Vedas, officer, the beginning is the *Aditya Hridaya stotram*.

> *"Tato yuddha parishraantam samarechintaya asthitam*
> *Raavanam jaagrato drishtavayuddha ayasam upasthitam."*

This hymn is to glorify the Sun god. As per the legend, this hymn was taught to Lord Ram by the cosmic sage Agastya before his epic battle with the demon king Ravana. The demon king had conquered all the worlds and the sage knew it was possible to kill him only if the sun god gave him the needed energy."

Lance was itching to interrupt, but Abinay signalled him not to. Because he knew his father did not like to be cut while he spoke. The old man continued, "Then there are verses from the *Bhagvad Gita*, it says, "The supreme godhead, that is the greatest reservoir of all material opulence, holds only quarter of the lord's energy. The rest of the three-fourth of the energy in the spiritual world is seen as dark energy by scientists, because of its unknown nature.

"Officer, the author of this document goes on to say, the one-fourth of the lord's energy includes all the material realm, even the outer space, that is vastly unknown to us. That this one-fourth energy described in the Gita, resulted in the creation of the universe. *Nasadiya Sukta* or as the western world translates it as 'The Hymn of Creation' corresponds to the modern-day Big Bang theory."

Lance couldn't stop himself from intervening this time around, and before he could be stopped, he blurted out, "Big Bang theory is scientifically proven concept sir, no one can deny this fact, whereas these ancient texts are only mythical."

Narsimha Chaturvedi cynically smiled and caressing his short ponytail on his otherwise shaven head spoke, his voice cold, "I know for a fact that you, officer Abinay, do not have faith in ancient Indian knowledge. Looks like your colleague too is like you. Not your mistake, though. The world was ignorant for a long time, but ancient Indian texts gained global prominence in the 18th century after which space agencies like NASA and ESA began revering the ancient texts. It is unfortunate that we ourselves aren't believers and custodians of the greatest sources of knowledge we possess!

"The day we disregarded our ancient knowledge, we started decaying as a society. We must not forget that the difference between us, humans and any other living form is the knowledge that our ancestors preserved for us, accompanied with the instinct to learn and expand it.

"Now, coming back to the Hymn of Creation, how does it correspond to the Big Bang theory? Let me explain. The hymn begins with the description of what existed before the creation of the universe. There was no sky, no air and no water. No one can tell what it was, where it was and what covered it. In the classic Big Bang theory, this state is called 'Singularity'.

"The hymn further describes the nature of singularity. In terms of the modern-day Big Bang theory, the universe is thought to have begun from an infinitesimal, vibrant, self-sustaining and intensely dense singularity. But there is no explanation in the Big Bang theory about the origin of singularity.

"The Big Bang theory assumes singularity existed in black holes in eternal darkness and intense heat. The Hymn of Creation, on the other hand, much before the modern theory was proposed described that it was darkness, void and formless. From which was born a great power of warmth.

"As the *Nasadiya Sukta* explains in the verse further, the actual explosion or the big bang was triggered by momentary desire, a primal seed of spirit. As described in the modern-day Big Bang theory, the explosion was triggered at a point when Singularity underwent a brief moment of inflation. It expanded faster than the speed of light, it increased more than a hundred times of its original size. Needless to say, it continued to expand and slowly cooled to form the current universe.

"Then the hymn describes thousands of years ago what modern scientists have discovered very recently. It says no one can conclusively prove anything about the Big Bang theory. Einstein's theory of relativity talks about Singularity. But modern scientists deny the theory on the grounds of Quantum Mechanics. To bring back what the Hymn of Creation states – the very beginning of the universe remains murky.

"The hymn concludes with a self-explanatory verse, that states that even the first born of this creation did not know about the creation of the universe. It is hard to comprehend by any human mind and impossible to conclusively prove by any living being."

As Narsimha Chaturvedi finished his narration, Abinay rose to fetch his father a glass of water. But Lance was too curious to know further, he could hardly wait for the elderly man to gulp the water in his hand. As soon as he kept the glass on the floor, Lance was addressing him with a probing question.

"Is that all that is written? How is anything you said related to the man getting killed?"

Abinay gave his subordinate a cold stare, letting him know that he needed to hold his horses for a bit. In a moment Mr Chaturvedi spoke again, "Hold on officer, I have more to tell you. But what I tell you, would it help in finding the culprit, you need it to figure that out.

Lance sat back with a sheepish smile on his face.

"Sarvepa avoyadagnil tasmedagnaupa avoramante"

"The author of this text has indeed done a lot of ground work. After dissecting the *Nasadiya Sukta,* he now relates it to this Sanskrit verse. The verse translates to – all matter particles are transformed from energy, so it may be said that all particles reside in energy.

"In modern science, this verse could be closely related to the first law of thermodynamics. The law states, energy can neither be created nor can it be destroyed. Energy can only be transformed from one form to another. He goes on to say if the universe was the result of something as minute as the singularity, unthinkable amount of energy can be extracted from space.

"Dwelling deeper into the concept he quotes, the sun as the purest and most long-lasting source of energy that inhabitants of earth can leverage. He says the device he has visualized and designed can source enough energy to not only end the energy crisis the world is facing, but also make us the undisputed kings of the world."

"But you will have to take a little more trouble to help us. You will have to take us through all the data in those files. I am sure Yuyutsu must have explained more about the device he has designed," Abinay said.

"Yes, he has, and don't worry I will take you through all the text. Let us continue... In the text in continuation to the Hymn of Creation the scientist further digs into the idea of actually harnessing 100% energy from a star. The sun in this case, quoting the concept of the scientific civilizations he further explains…

"We, as a living planet are currently a type I civilization, this means we as a planet are utilizing all the energy of the planet. In a type II civilization, the entire energy is an output of a star. A type III civilization is where the energy output of an entire galaxy is harnessed. He then says, even if we can build the capability of becoming a type II civilization, we can solve our energy crisis for centuries."

Once again Lance jumped forward with his typical comments, "Perhaps, you are right, sir. We might clean up our oceans, reverse global warming, turn iron to gold or do any number of such activities. Fossil fuels cannot suffice our growing demands of energy in the first place. Even if they do, they come with many undesirable side effects."

He went on without waiting for an answer, "But sir, has he written anything about how he thinks achieving a type II civilization will be possible?"

"ekaevaagnirbahudhesamiddhai"

"This verse again reiterates the *Nasadiya Sukta* or Hymn of Creation. It says all visible material particles are made up of energy. Also remember, in *Yajurveda, Ashva* translated to as a horse in Sanskrit, is also referred to be the sun as it is the primary source of energy.

"The Puranas talk about the Ashvamedha Yagna, which is a process of harnessing the solar energy. Undisputed kings in ancient India performed it for sustenance of life on earth. The *rishis* and scholars of ancient India, by the virtue of their wisdom harnessed the solar energy to achieve various technological tasks."

Lance interrupted sarcastically once again, "Technology and five thousand years ago…?"

"Yes officer, why not? Haven't you heard or read about Karna's invincible armour and earrings? His mother Kunti was blessed by the Sun god and Karna was born wearing the armor and earrings. Both the armor and the earrings were received 'energy' from the sun, that protected him from any weapon!"

This time it was Abinay who was about to put his hand up in clarification, but before he could…

"I know what you are going to say, officer. Isn't it about the Mahabharata being just a legendry epic? Even if that is true and you believe such armors and earrings, or any other such things are only mythical, gentlemen, have you heard of Oppenheimer?"

Lance responded, surprising his chief for a change, "Are you talking about J.Robert Oppenheimer? Often called the father of the atomic bomb?"

"Yes officer, you are right. You might not know but even Oppenheimer believed the *Bhagvad Gita,* if we go by that belief all the characters of the epic existed in flesh and blood and also had extraordinary powers. The Pentagon is trying to mimic Karna's armor and earrings with Nano-suites. The *Yajurveda,* that sheds ample amount of light on generation of energy in the sun, clearly states that protons, which are positively charged particles, can catalyze or quicken the continuous generation of energy in the sun.

"Now returning to the topic of a type II civilization and the device design, Yuyutsu begins by saying, a Dyson Sphere or a cloud could be built to collect all the solar energy that emanates from it. Before any of you ask, I'll briefly explain what a Dyson Sphere is.

"A Dyson Sphere is a hypothetical megastructure that encircles a star. These are considered to be a sign of extraterrestrial astronomers or other intelligent beings in outer space."

"Has anything like this been observed in the past, sir?"

"A handful of researchers mapped the night sky. But didn't see anything out of the ordinary for a long time. But in 2015 an astronomer Tebetha Boyajian reported the mysterious dimming of a star. This irregular flickering was something that awed the scientific community and was suspected to be a Dyson Sphere. The star was named Tabby's star in the astronomer's honour.

"But here, Yuyutsu goes on to be assertive that as an intelligent species the human race can do much better than just the Dyson Sphere! That is to extract material directly from the star. He dwells into an idea called Stellar Lifting. It is the concept of stealing hydrogen from the sun, store it and using it for generation of our futuristic energy.

"The sun is actually spewing hydrogen naturally, which can be collected at the lagrange point between the sun and earth. The collected hydrogen can be used for generating energy. The scientist writes, the ejection of hydrogen has to be increased and the device he was building is capable of exactly that.

"He further explains the working of his device called The Collider. It is designed like a long tube of thousands of superconducting magnets. In the forefront of the tube, there is a clock like dial, over which attached are blades that look like fan blades.

"These electromagnets are built using special electric cables that operate in super conducting state without resistance or any loss of energy. This requires cold temperatures of -271 degrees Celsius or below. These thousands of magnets can direct the beams of hydrogen atomic particles. Just before the collision, another kind of magnet helps to squeeze the tiny particles to increase the chances of their contact.

"The collision like this, that is conducted in such a charged electric environment in super cold temperatures, is capable of creating unimaginable energy sphere that can suck anything into it. It returns whatever goes in along with enormous spurts of energy."

"But, how can all the hydrogen reach earth from the sun? Isn't the sun millions of kilometres away?"

"You are right son, the scientist has indeed clarified your doubt. Because the hydrogen cannot be brought to earth to harness energy, the collider must be placed in the lagrange between the sun and the earth."

"What is a lagrange now? Is it some kind of parking space in outer space, where he proposes to park his device, the collider?" snapped Lance!

"It is exactly what you are saying officer. The lagrange points are locations in space where the gravitational forces between large bodies like the sun and the earth or the earth and the moon are equal. The interaction of these forces creates equilibrium, where spacecrafts along with loaded devices can be parked."

"Sir, the relation of Vedic astronomy and the device Yuyutsu designed or even was building could only be theoretical, for all we know. Can anything that could defy such great forces of gravity be really made in real? I know there are references of Shivakar Talpade inventing the airplane before the Wright brothers, but is there anything else?"

Lance observed the old man scratch his stubble mildly. A habit probably his son had picked from the father. He couldn't help a spontaneous, but momentary smile. He thanked his stars that both father and son were lost in deep thought and did not notice him having his bit of fun. After a long moment of thought, the old man spoke, "Yes, my son, there are many such examples where Vedic knowledge has served in the forefront for the betterment of humanity. I shall tell you a few. The Hymn of Creation is a prime example of the same. All the secrets of the universe lie in the womb of the *Nasadiya Sukta*.

"But to answer your question in particular, ancient Indians were capable of more than just inventing aircrafts. They had achieved much more amazing and unbelievable things. Many researchers talk about UFOs and alien sightings and have gone on record saying that the ancient Vedic scriptures refer to aeronautics, spaceships, flying machines and ancient astronauts.

"Soviet scientists in the past had found age-old vehicles of cosmic navigation in caves of Turkestan and Gobi Desert. These are hemispherical objects that resemble the description of flying machines in ancient scriptures. It was evident the ancient Indian astronauts travelled across the world in these machines.

"Another amazing prospect that researchers and historians bring to light is the propulsion theory of these incredible flying machines. The method of propulsion was anti-gravitational and was based on a system of Laghima."

Lance looked at Abinay, he seemed confused, and before Mr Chaturvedi could continue, "Laghima, my dear friend, is one of the eight super human capabilities than can be achieved by the most disciplined practice of the *ashta siddhi* or the eight-fold *yoga*. It is an ability by which one can become almost weightless. According to Hindu yogis it is Laghima which enables one to levitate."

Abinay then looked at his father, requesting him to add more details.

"You are right, Abinay. Once anyone masters the eight-fold yogic practices and realizes the capabilities mentioned by Abinay, they can alter a perceived object and bend them as they like. They can regroup the composition of matter, make things very light. Even make things move in vacuum."

"But sir, if all that you are saying is true, where did all that knowledge go? Didn't any of these yogis who mastered the eight-fold yoga document their work? Didn't they realize the worth of it?"

"They did and that is why archeologists have found scriptures over the decades. But yes, many were either lost or could be hidden."

"Hidden! Why would anyone hide such great knowledge, sir?" Lance asked a little irritated.

"I am not a historian, but the little reading I have done and thanks to the few experts I met, I have learnt a little. During the time that Ashoka reigned over the land mass of the Indian subcontinent…"

Lance interrupted, "Sir, are you referring to the two thousand-year-old secret society of the nine unknown men who wrote nine books on different subjects? Coincidentally I have read and heard that one of the nine books dealt with gravity control!"

A spark of intrigue suddenly ignited in the old man's eyes.

"Are you also a believer in the existence of the secret society?"

Lance looked at Abinay for an answer, who intervened instantly, "The answer is related to the details of the murder case we are investigating. Hence, we cannot discuss it. But please tell us if you know anything more about the society and any documentation related to them. Please feel no offense."

"I surely understand, son, and I will also share what I know. I remember reading about an age-old text written in Sanskrit on palm leaves that was discovered in Lhasa, Tibet and was sent to the University of Chandigarh. Experts who looked at these palm leaves were very excited to realize that the text contained instructions about constructing an interstellar spaceship."

"Could it be possible that the set of palm leaves discovered in Tibet was indeed the same book written by one of the nine unknown men of Ashoka? There is no proven evidence, but there have been instances that point towards the same.

"Records have been found that during 1930s, almost a decade before World War II, Adolf Hitler and his Nazi staff developed great interest in ancient India and Tibet. Expeditions were sent to both these countries, in order to gather the esoteric knowledge and evidence of secret hymns from the Vedas to explore and learn.

"Unfortunately, that same knowledge was used to build weapons of tremendous mass destruction. In fact it is interesting to know that Nazis were the first to build engines for 'Buzz Bombs' that they used in the war. It is sad that we as a nation and civilization failed to realize the power of these ancient scriptures. But others did, for the wrong reasons!"

The old man's voice cracked in disappointment as he spoke his last sentence. Abinay noticed the sudden change in his father's tone.

"What is wrong, Dad? Why is there a sudden cloud of gloom on your face? Are you not feeling well?"

Lance saw the softer side of his superior the moment sadness clouted his father's face. He had addressed his father as Dad and not sir, and attended to him as a caring and loving son.

"I am okay, son, you need not worry about me. It is just that I am saddened that the author of this document too was chasing the materialistic power the knowledge could have given him. Despite his deep understanding of these scriptures, he failed to understand that the real purpose of these powers was to serve the society and not personal gain.

"Yes son, I feel so because the hunger of power is evident. The line that differentiates knowledge from wisdom is very thin. Wisdom does not crave for power, but knowledge does. This very craving might be the reason for his death. It made me feel sad that an intellect of his standing thought like this."

"You are right, Dad. That indeed is disappointing. But we are grateful to you for helping us understand the text in these documents. The understanding has given our investigation a new direction. Thank you very much, but we might come back to trouble you."

"Yathasikhamayuranamnaganam manayoyatha,
Tadvadvedangusastranamjyotisam (ganitam)
murdhanisthitam."

Lance smirked, "Why does the old man throw punch lines in Sanskrit? He knows I don't understand the language!"

Abinay patted his assistant on the shoulders, calming him down. Then he translated his father's words.

"Like the crests on the heads of peacocks, like the gems on the hoods of the cobras, Astronomy (Mathematics) is at the top of the Vedanga *shastras* – the auxiliary branches of the Vedic knowledge."

"I am always be happy to help, son! You can come whenever you need help. Always remember that."

The two young men walked out with a new zeal of hope.

"Chief, now do we go the ISA chairman's office?" Lance asked eager to know the next move!

"Yes! We shall go to the ISA chief and then analyze the evidences we found at Manas's residence."

▼

At the ISA office later, both men barged into the chief's cabin, "Apologies sir, but I need to interrupt the very important discussions you might be having. Because I believe I have something more important to talk about."

The chief scientist looked at Abinay, not very amused. He sighed deeply and told the others around him, "Gentlemen, looks like we will have to continue our discussion after a short break. The cop has something important."

The chief scientist scoffed at Abinay, the other scientists took the cue and left the cabin, murmuring in scuffled voices.

"Sir, I am here because we have found some new evidences related to Yuyutsu Ghosh's alleged murder. I need to ask you some questions."

"But I have already had one round of interrogation and I have already told your subordinate everything I knew. I don't know what more you want to know, officer?"

Scratching his stubble, Abinay stepped closer to the table that separated the two men.

"Did you know about the solar devise Yuyutsu was building or the project he was working on?"

The chief scientist rose from his chair, pushed his spectacles up his nose and spoke, "I have answered this question before too officer. Yuyutsu was serving his notice period, so we had not assigned him any project. Moreover, he had spoilt relations with all of us, why will he share any details of his work?"

Then he asked, "But did you mention a solar project?"

The scientist's voice suddenly turned concerned and he slumped into his chair.

"Yes! Do you know anything about it?"

"Not in detail, but he had come to me with a project proposal regarding the device. I did not think it was a feasible and realistic project. He got offended and the argument got a little bitter."

"That is when this insult episode unfolded itself, isn't it? But why did you folks think Yuyutsu's proposal made no sense?"

"His proposal was to build a hydrogen collider and send it to the lagrange points in outer space where hydrogen spews from the sun. This is only a theoretical concept; it cannot be realized. Because such a system can become highly unstable and create a hostile situation. The kind of enormous energy this device can generate is extremely difficult to control, even in a testing phase. Hence, investing the tax payers' money in such unrealistic misadventures isn't practical or safe.

"I know, as a scientist I should have believed in possibilities of science and been optimistic. But this idea seemed to work only in sci-fi comics, so I did not encourage Yuyutsu."

A sarcastic smile widened on Abinay's face, his eyes had a look of disdain. As he tapped his fingers on the table rising to his feet, the scientist continued, "Yuyutsu wasn't ready to accept these facts and got offended and things got out of hand. I wish they hadn't, now I regret I did not get an opportunity to mend the spoilt friendship."

Abinay did not comment and he left the ISA chief's office without a word, "Come on Lance, we shall figure out the truth ourselves!"

Abinay stormed out of the cabin and Lance followed him. An hour later, both men were staring at the computer screen on Abinay's table. They were looking at the image of the text file recovered from Yuyutsu's hard disk and Abinay was making certain calculations scribbling on a sheet of paper. On top was written, "CEDBEAECBCEAEABDBAEDAEABADCBCBDBAA"

"12131345134523234331112"

Below which he had scribble some calculations and as he did so, Lance kept toggling between the computer screen and the paper Abinay was scribbling on. Lance had always been interested in hard-core action. Hence, his interests always remained in police routines and not in the analysis and problem-solving activities. He now had to wait for Abinay to explain what he was doing.

Finally, he wrote, "THE SMILING BUDDHA and "BCCUCUHHSLB"

"Chief, what is all this scribbling you have done and then you finally end up with smiling Buddha! I am not able to connect the dots."

"Not the right time to answer your questions. We have a more important puzzles to solve.

Lance did not understand the sudden excitement on Abinay's face. Abinay told Lance, "I have deciphered the encrypted bunch of characters we found in Yuyutsu's hard disk. The decryption is "THE SMILING BUDDHA", but what is it referring to? Why was this hard disk so well encrypted to guard a small message? Moreover, where can I find this smiling Buddha?"

As Abinay sat in his cabin lost in thought, Lance left to have a check on the chemical test results run on the air-condition particles collected. By the time he walked back into the cabin to let his superior that the AC sample tested positive for the presence of Ricin, Abinay had spread all the pictures taken by his investigation team in front of him. Suddenly, Abinay rushed to Lance; he was holding a picture of a wall that had a smiling Buddha painted on it.

"Come on Lance, we need to go to Manas's house immediately. I think I have found the smiling Buddha that was being referred to in the encrypted file."

Lance was lost. He couldn't figure out anything Abinay was saying. He only understood they had to go.

"Let us go, I'll explain everything on the way!"

While he drove, Abinay spoke, "While you were checking on the chemical test results, I looked at the pictures taken of the crime scene as part of investigation. What I found was this picture that blew my mind. How could I not think of it earlier? This picture is of one of the walls in Manas's house. If you notice, this painting is the smiling Buddha.

"We need to check it out, we cannot neglect any clue. I have a hunch we might get a breakthrough from the wall."

Abinay understood that Lance was still not completely convinced, "What is disturbing you, Lance?"

"Chief, how did you figure the clue from the encrypted message? Please explain..."

"The message we recovered from the hard disk was encrypted using the Polybius Square cipher. It can be detected if there are only 5 to 6 characters used in the cipher text. It is very similar to the simple substitution cipher, the only difference being that each plain text is enciphered with two characters.

"This algorithm offers very less communication security and can be broken easily. I guess Yuyutsu wasn't satisfied with the encryption he had built for the secret and that is why he asked Rahul to encrypt his hard disk."

"Chief, could this also mean that Yuyutsu and Manas were in touch with each other?"

"That is a very strong possibility, Lance, but what could a space scientist and a neuroscientist be working on together?"

Both men reached the crime scene with so many questions in their head. But answers for none of them and they were sure the Buddha will answer many of these questions.

The house was well secured by policemen who were put on duty. Abinay and Lance entered the house and went into the master bedroom as mentioned in the picture. The painting seemed very common. Abinay walked up to the wall to take a closer look at the painting. Rather, the wall. Everything seemed normal. Abinay started to feel the wall with his hands. As he passed the eyes of the painting, he realized a hollow in there.

Abinay moved his fingers again over the eyes of the smiling Buddha and as it was hollow, he tried pressing it as if the smiling Buddha was holding a great secret in his chest. The eyes were the latches that unlocked the chest of the painting. From within came out an iron hand, in its palm was embedded a fingerprint scanner.

"I thought as much..."

Abinay murmured, then took his mobile out and called Dr Pashupathi, "Doctor, as I predicted, Manas has used biometrics to protect some data. What is the status of his fingerprint moulds? I need them as soon as possible."

"The process needs a few more hours, officer, I cannot hasten the making. By the way, which hand do you need? However, I am making the moulds for both. I am sure you'd know that most biometric systems would have pre-set number of attempts to unlock them, post which they might self-destruct, and the data protected in them can be lost forever!"

"I'd need your help to decide that, doctor. I'll try and fetch a hand written document, probably a signed document. If you could analyze his writing and tell us if he was a right hander or left, as you are a handwriting expert, then I will make an educated guess about which finger's mould to use to unlock the system."

Lance was waiting for Abinay to finish the conversation and then queried, "Chief, why do you ask for a handwriting analysis? How would it help?"

Abinay patted Lance on his shoulder, smiled and spoke, "It is for a calculated risk we need to take, my friend. Many a time investigation's successes depend on gut feelings and instincts. Let me explain, take out your mobile phone and unlock it."

Lance did as he was asked to.

"You unlocked your phone using your right-hand thumb's fingerprint, because you are a right hander. That is what most people would do. Use their thumb or index finger to lock and unlock their phones. Now once we analyze Manas's signature and figure out his active hand, we can make an educated guess about which finger he might have used to lock the biometric. Yes, it is risky, but gut feel is an important factor in the success of investigations."

The two men ran an extensive search in the house for a hand-written document. Finally they found torn pieces of an expired cheque leaf in the dustbin.

"Lance, hand over this torn cheque leaf to Dr Pashupathi and ask him to analyze the signature. Meanwhile I shall ask the officers on duty to secure the crime scene."

Abinay walked to the gate where two constables stood on duty. Both anticipated trouble since the moment Abinay had visited, they knew he would ask them tough questions. He would have expected them to give him some vital information. But they had nothing to tell him, hence they were nervous. They looked at each other with blank expressions as Abinay approached them, not sure what to expect.

"Gentlemen, did you see anything suspicious in the past few day that you have been posted here?"

Both men shook their heads. Looking at their blank faces, Abinay held his nerve and calmed himself stalling the raging storm within. After a moment of silence and thought, he paraphrased his question trying to sound more pointed and specific.

"Did you notice anyone wearing a jacket designed with nine spokes, a wheel and a lion face in its centre?"

As expected, he did not get any useful response from his subordinates. But a favourable response came from an unexpected source. Someone patted Abinay on his shoulder from behind. He turned to look at a middle-aged woman dressed in a lose shirt, pajama and a pair of floaters. The woman wore an equally confused expression on her face, as there was on Abinay's face. Finally swallowing the disgust his men had made him feel and trying his best to keep calm, Abinay said, “Yes, ma’am, how can I help you?”

Looking at those intense eyes, the woman felt overwhelmed and at a loss for words. Looking at her struggling to speak, Abinay’s tone softened.

“Are you alright? Do you need some water?”

One of the men standing behind took the cue and offered some water to her. After reassuring her well-being, he asked, “Ma’am, did you sense any danger? Was anyone following you? Don’t worry, you are safe now. My men will escort you home.”

The two men started to walk the woman home, suddenly she found her voice and blurted out, “The lion-faced jacket!”

Stunned at what he heard, Abinay turned around, the intensity was back in his eyes. But he made sure his voice remained as calm as possible.

“What did you say, ma’am? How do you know about the jacket? Did you see anyone wearing it around this place? Don’t be anxious. I don’t mean harm to you, but the lead you give me will help save lives. Please tell me what you saw or know.”

The woman calmed down at Abinay’s request and then spoke, “Yes officer, I did see a man with the jacket and the design you are talking about. This was five days ago, I remember vividly.”

Abinay’s curiosity aroused, he narrowed his eyes and continued questioning, but keeping his voice and response calm enough.

“What makes you remember him so vividly? Could you explain what happened?”

“It was actually my husband who was bringing some groceries. This guy wearing the jacket had covered his face with a funny looking mask and bumped into my husband and started a quarrel. It was right here at this gate and my house is just a few blocks away. My husband is a cranky and hot-tempered person, so he got angry and let his hands lose on the guy.

"The guy's funny outfit made my husband believe that he was a crook. Looking at the crowd gathering, probably the guy chickened out and fled to save himself. The next day, the residents of this house were found dead and the house was cordoned off by your men. My husband didn't want us to get into trouble, so we didn't report. Though I wanted to, but now seeing you here, I thought I must report that I suspect that guy's involvement in the death of the residents."

"Yes ma'am, he is the prime suspect. You should have reported earlier, however, thank you for doing so now. My team will reach out to you to testify, if needed. You may go now, my men will escort you."

▼

Abinay then reached Dr Pashupathi's office where the doctor was working on the piece of paper Lance had given him. Lance himself was watching the man, perplexed.

"Sorry doctor, I feel bad to put you through this at this late hour. I wouldn't have bothered you it wasn't as important."

"The day I got involved in this case and I got to know you were the IO, I knew I am going to live with long working nights, officer. I was mentally prepared, don't worry." The doctor responded laughing out loud.

"Here you go! I have analyzed the signature, assuming it is Manas's. It's a right-hander's sign. I cannot confirm this is

Manas's because this is the only sample we have, and we cannot make him sign now. As far as the fingerprint moulds you asked for, they are ready. These work nine out of ten times, provided you choose the right finger."

"Thank you, doctor!"

The two cops left the doctor's office, hoping they have gotten a step closer to solving the mystery. But they knew only time would tell if they really were or not. As Lance drove back to Manas's residence, Abinay asked, "Lance, we couldn't discuss the AC sample test results. What did you find out?"

"Yes chief, the tests are positive!"

"That is great, my friend. The suspect with the jacket was also seen near the crime scene a day before the crime happened. This indicates that he is still our prime suspect. Now if we open the secret locker, we shall be another step closer to solving this mystery."

The two men reached the crime scene quickly, as there was less traffic at night. They got to the painting on the wall, pressed the buttons in the eyes of the painting. The fingerprint scanner surfaced from its chest. Thankfully, unlocking it was as smooth as traversing a knife through butter. It was the thumb fingerprint that deactivated the lock.

To the surprise of the two men, this time the wall turned itself into a cabinet. When it was opened, a folder full of papers was found, the language used was Sanskrit. With the limited Sanskrit he knew, Abinay figured out that the files contained details about the human brain.

He wondered where this case was going. As if he was lost in a desert, chasing a mirage. Each time there was a glimmer of hope of finding a big breakthrough, it was followed by such a twist, that he was back to square one. After a slight pause, the two men picked the file from the cabinet, set everything back as if nothing had changed.

Back in his cabin, Abinay sat alone, studying the file they had recovered from the secret cabinet in Manas's house. Abinay had asked Lance to go home and rest as they were going to be having a busy day ahead. As he screened through the file, he noticed something that caught his attention. It was a series of digits that seemed familiar. When he took a closer look, he realized that it was the same series that was found in Yuyutsu's hard disk.

Abinay looked at his watch; it was quite late. He dropped a text to Dr Pashupathi, checking on the forensic report of the skeleton found in the dungeon of Manas's house. Then he texted Manish to share the decryption of number series found with the "THE SMILING BUDDHA" message. Then he rested his head on the desk and did not realize when he dozed off. A couple of hours rolled by. It was early in the morning; the day had just broken. He dialled his father's number, who had just finished his morning prayer.

"Tell me son, what makes you call me so early in the morning? Is everything ok?"

"Yes, Dad, everything is alright. I found a lead in the case in another Sanskrit document. It talks about the human brain. I remember one of your friends is an ayurvedic doctor who has spent a lot of time researching about the brain. I need you to ask him to help me with these documents. I could have used official power, but I don't want to."

"I understand son, his name is Brahaspathi. It is better I try and talk to him because he is kind of a detached character. Sometimes one might mistake his detachment with irritability. We will not know what can trigger his temper off the roof, but everything said and done, he still is a very learned man. You come over and I shall take you to him."

Lance and Abinay were driving to Bhrahaspathi's house after picking up his father from his place. That's when Abinay's mobile beeped, indicating a text he had received from Dr Pashupathi. It read, "Working on the skeleton, shall give you details by tonight."

Abinay had kept his phone back in his pocket, it beeped again. This time it was Manish, who had dropped a message, saying he would try to find out more on the decrypted text sent to him. That's when Narsimha Chaturvedi warned them, "I suggest both of you switch off your phones, conversations with Brahaspathi could get very tricky. He only talks to people when he feels like doing so, he doesn't have long conversations in the first place. When he has a conversation, he must not be interrupted. You never know when he will walk out. Make sure you let him lead the conversation. More importantly, do not let your egos accompany you to see him."

The trio reached Bhrahaspathi's house. It was a small country house, built in the middle of a farm. The trio were supposed to walk into the house through an open door, as if they were expected. But before they did, a firm voice from the inside of the house asked them to leave their footwear out. The trio did as they were asked to. When they walked in, they saw a man in his sixties, sitting on the floor surrounded by a sea of books.

Without getting distracted from what he was reading, he indicated to his visitors to make themselves comfortable. There were no chairs or mattresses around, so all three sat on the floor folding their legs. After a while, Bhrahaspathi closed the book he was reading and spoke with the most curt and coldest voice ever, "Tell me, Chaturvedi, what brings you to me? You know I don't like visitors. I only let you come because I know you would have a genuine reason! Make it fast, I don't like my house being crowded."

"Sure, Bhrahaspathi… I brought my son and his friend. They are police officers. They need help in solving a criminal case."

"Criminal case! Are these officers accusing me of any crime? Are they going to interrogate me?"

There was a sudden spunk of defiance in his voice, at which Abinay responded very humbly, "Sir, please don't misunderstand our intent. We are not here to cause any trouble to you. But we are here because we need help in solving this case and possibly save lives. We would remain indebted to you for your help!"

The anger in the old man's eyes disappeared suddenly, his face softened. Bhrahaspathi felt moved by the humility Abinay had acted with. He hadn't expected a cop exhibit such emotions.

"Alright son, tell me how I can help you?"

Lance was about to sing a few praises of the old man. But Abinay had caught his pulse and signalled him not to. He quietly handed the copies of documents that were recovered from the secret cabinet and sat down waiting to hear from the old man.

Hours rolled by, but there was no word from him. He had buried himself in the pile of study material. He was toggling between the content Abinay gave him, various technical journals, international news clippings and neurology books. Lance, after a while started getting jittery. He murmured, "Chief, what is going on? Do you think this old man can lead us anywhere? Manas Parthasarthi was a neuroscientist, dealing with complex research on the human brain. Here we have an old-school Ayurveda follower. I really think we are in the wrong place."

Abinay patted on his thighs, "Don't worry Lance, this guy isn't just an Ayurveda follower. His pet project has been the human brain and he has done extensive research for the last two decades. Not only that, father tells me that he is up-to-date with international research advancements around the globe. I am sure he will not send us empty-handed."

Finally, after some more wait, Bhrahaspathi spoke, "The mind, my friends, is nothing but a bundle of subtle desires. It is just like a cloth, a bundle of threads, a bunch of past impressions that permanently lurk around the sub-conscious. When the threads of a cloth are pulled out one-by-one, is anything of the cloth left? Similarly, when all the desires are destroyed, along with their seeds, the mind reaches a state of self-realization and becomes immortal.

"But one has to traverse through several phases to reach that supreme state of awareness and spiritual consciousness. Such an epitome of self-realized and enlightened state of the mind is called the *bhramakara-vritti*. Many fail to overcome the trap of worldly attractions and remain entrapped in the pursuit of materialistic goals.

"The mind is the source of the wishes of all these pursuits. It is also a more powerful weapon than all the weapons in the world put together. The powers of the mind are indescribable and unimaginable! Terrific powers and psychic abilities are mere expressions of the mind as it nears the all-powerful consciousness. These are yogic powers that some individuals use for selfish gains, making these powers dreadful.

"The literature you have recovered talks about one such super power, 'immortality'. The best part is that this description takes an entirely different approach. Similarities can be drawn between this literature and ancient Vedic scriptures. The only difference here is that the author of this document speaks about achieving immortality digitally."

The three men sat up erect as the subject triggered their curiosities. But they kept their mouths shut, as they didn't want to annoy the old man. But there were questions in all their minds, written all over their faces.

Bhrahaspathi continued, "Let's do this a little differently, let's reverse engineer. We will talk about what is described here in your literature and then I'll help you relate that with the Vedas. That way, you can try and stay with me as I connect the dots."

There was pin drop silence in the room. The old man took it as consent and spoke again, "Scientists around the world believe that we are a few decades away of having digital versions of ourselves. But your friend here has other ideas. If we were to believe his claim, he was in the final stages of achieving what could be called 'Virtual Immortality'.

"He claims that the technology he is at the verge of delivering will have the capability of generating holograms to digitize human consciousness. This man is not just a neuroscientist, but seems to be a bio-technologist too. He claims to have developed a futuristic technology that will be an emulation of oneself. In other words, the creation of a cyber self.

"He seems to have figured it all here, calls it the Avatar project. According to the design, developing a robot that can be controlled by the human brain was Avatar A, the first of the four phases. Avatar B involved transplanting a synthetic brain into a synthetic body. Uploading the content of a biological brain to a synthetic one is the third phase. The fourth and final phase of his Avatar project relies on emulation. That is replacing the biological brain and body with a hologram as a host to the human consciousness.

"Gentlemen, if the claims are to be considered true and the project has indeed gone through or was going through any of them… if life-like avatars have been or were being developed, a lot of ground work must have been done. The structure of the brain needs to be mapped. There are about a hundred and thirty billion neurons in a human brain and each one of them is connected to the rest in a complex neural network.

"These connections and their functions need to be deciphered. The electric signals need to be translated to code. Last but not the least, a physical hardware needs to be developed to achieve immortalization.

Lance could no longer hold his curiosity and burst out, "The stuff written in these pages doesn't make any sense. Are we living in a mythical world? How can anyone be immortal?"

Narsimha Chaturvedi hit his palm on his forehead in utter disgust. He was almost certain that this outburst from Lance would have irritated Bhrahaspathi. He would definitely stop the read-out now. But strangely enough, the old man did not lose temper. He smiled and continued, making all three men curious,

"Do not fret gentlemen, what has been described here is very much possible. Many veteran scientists, most notably inventor Ray Kurzweil has extensively written about this concept. Neuroscientists and bio-technologists globally have collaborated to work on a project called 'The Blue Brain'. The goal of this project is to biologically reconstruct and simulate the brain of a rodent and ultimately a human brain."

Bhrahaspathi was continuing in his own merry way. He was totally immersed in the topic at hand. That is when Abinay's father realized the reason why the Ayurveda expert wasn't perturbed when Lance blurted out instinctively.

"Even if you believe that all that I told you is out of a science fiction novel and can be possible only in an author's imagination, there are technologies that were considered impossible just a few years ago. These are household names now, and even school kids talk about them. I will not be surprised if a few years from now, we find a digital version of people."

Abinay realized at that moment, it was all French and Latin to Lance. It was best he intervened to assure to his subordinate that the old man was still making sense. He rose to his feet and with utmost humility spoke, "Sir, my apologies to interrupt in between your detailed explanation. If I might ask, are you referring to artificial intelligence and machine learning?"

Bhrahaspathi nodded, acknowledging the accuracy and clarity in Abinay's thoughts. He appreciated the fact that he was open to learning things that were beyond his job.

"Yes, young man, that is exactly what I am talking about. Artificial intelligence and machine learning in the modern-day world are no more a fantasy or luxury. Revolutionary advancements are happening in the world of technology. There is no surprise if virtual humanity becomes reality soon. Why go far? Look at your iPhones, isn't SIRI (Speech Interpretation and Recognition Interface), Apple's path breaking virtual voice assistance system, a part of your lives already?"

"The rise in autonomy being given to computer-controlled systems represent nothing but a steady shift in artificial intelligence. This infact is the infant stage of digital immortalization in the true sense.

"But the immortality the Vedas speak about was much more advanced. According to the Vedas, immortality could be achieved directly. Some worthy people had activated the power of their minds that they could keep themselves alive for as long as they wished for."

"Sir, are you referring to the legend of the celibate Bheeshma about whom the epic *Mahabharata* speaks of?" The character who vowed that he would neither claim his right to the throne, nor get married and raise a family. All this so that his father could marry the woman of his dreams.

"Overwhelmed by the son's sacrifice, the father blessed the son with the power to command death to take his life only when he wished so!"

Bhrahaspathi's face bloomed into a knowing smile, "I knew you would refer to Bheeshma. But there are other great souls too, who have through their high-quality yogic lifestyle attained the ability to live just on the consumption of air. Just a single glance of such souls is rare. Only the blessed ones have gotten such opportunities. Those who did, have written commentaries about their experiences.

"There are written accounts describing the life of a saint who is living for over two thousand years, but looks only twenty-five. Fondly known as the 'Deathless Master', he is a descent of divinity into flesh. The dwarfed vision of man cannot comprehend his transcendental state, which is one of the reasons why the deathless master has never appeared publicly. He was the one who re-introduced the ancient science of *Kriya Yoga*. One who masters it can attain unbelievable powers of the mind and body. The deathless master is one such great soul which is lost because of man's indifference.

"The deathless master was well aware of the influence of the trend of modern times. The influence of change in thought process and the complexities it would cause. He realized the necessity of spreading self-liberation and yoga across the globe. The great soul has assisted several prophets in their special dispensations.

"In another first-hand account, it is confirmed that he remains in constant communion with Christ and both together send vibrations of redemption of this age. Hence, two illuminated souls, one with body, the other without it; work towards the spiritual healing of this world."

Bhrahaspathi finally finished his explanation, but there were question marks on Lance's face.

"I know what is troubling you. You want to know if I think digital immortality is a possible idea? You are also wondering about the consequences of such an invention in the society?

"To be honest with you, like many veteran scientists across the globe, I did not think digitizing humanity will be achieved in my lifetime. Though people all over the world are working towards immortality with multiple approaches, being able to achieve something of such a prospect was unimaginable.

"There is no doubt that it would be an exemplary achievement. The scientific community will hail the inventor, the world will reward him. But there is a very steep downside to it that not many will see. As far as I am concerned, I consider a breakthrough invention like the digital immortality or any other man-made way to achieve similar result against nature. Anything that is born has to die, remember the 'Circle of Life'?

"Let me explain, the only common certainty between every human with any socio-economic background is death! Now consider something like 'Digital Immortality' gets introduced. Certainly, it will be beyond the reach of the poor. This will result in social unrest in the society. That's when things will start to get crazy. This will lead to a race of creating a perfect breed, after eliminating the not-so-perfect beings."

"Eugenics! You are saying if immortality is achieved through any kind, it will lead to Eugenics?" Abinay asked as Bhrahaspathi ended his explanation.

Lance and Narsimha Chaturvedi looked at Abinay with a confused expression. Both couldn't relate to what the senior cop was referring to. The next moment, Bhrahaspathi walked to Chaturvedi and patted him on the back with a wide grin on his face. Abinay's father hadn't expected such a reaction from the old Ayurveda expert. He looked back even more confused.

"Your son is well read, Chaturvedi. I didn't expect a cop to know all the stuff he does. I'll let him explain Eugenics."

Abinay nodded and began, "Father, Eugenics in simple terms means selection of desirable heritable characteristics in order to improve future generations. The concept came into existence with the hope of giving the stronger races or strains of blood chances of prevailing over the weaker ones. Over time, the theory gained support of scientific communities and political leaders. Because it was based on the theory of 'Survival of the Fittest'. But the idea faded away when the Nazis took shelter to it and exterminated entire races."

"Not only that, Abinay," Bhrahaspathi added, "You can see Eugenics in India too."

"In India?" Suddenly Lance's curiosity sprang into action.

"Yes, in India! What do you think these honour killings happening across the country are? It is not just socio-economic inequality or caste differences causing these killings. Eugenics is a reason too! This would be bigger than any disaster in the world."

"Alright gentlemen! I have told you all I knew. I genuinely hope it helps you solve your case. Now I would want you to excuse me."

The three men got their cue that it was time for them to leave. They thanked the old man for his time and left.

For the first time in his career, Abinay was dealing with a case that was getting murkier as he dug deeper. For the first time he felt he had met his match in the culprit. Every layer he peeled off the case, it got ten-fold thicker. As he sat in the car thinking where his next lead would come from, Lance broke the silence, "Chief, one thing still bothers me from the explanation the old man gave."

"Go on, tell me what is it that bothers you?"

Lance took a deep breath and blurted out, "If the old man doesn't approve of digital immortality or any other man-made method to achieve similar results against nature, how can he approve the same concept if it is achieved through yogic lifestyle? Not only that, but also hail a godman as a great soul?"

"My friend, that is because it is believed that yogic lifestyle and Vedic study not only help one to attain extreme supernatural powers but also make sure the practitioner matures enough to understand the circle of life."

"In that case, why is the godman still keeping his human form? Is he beyond the circle of life?"

"I am no expert on this subject, Lance. But I'll tell you what I have heard from Dad. He used to tell me, no one is beyond the circle of life, not even gods. Anyone born as a mortal being has to cease to exist in that form, once the purpose of his or her existence is achieved. May be as Bhrahaspathi said, the great soul's purpose is not yet met."

As the two men continued their return journey to the headquarters, Abinay remembered that Dr Pashupathi and Manish might have tried to reach him. He instantly pulled his mobile phone out and switched it on. Only to see multiple missed calls and texts, asking him to return their calls. Lance too found his phone with similar outreach attempts. Abinay's first choice of returning the call was Dr Pashupathi.

"Dr Pashupathi, apologies I was held up, so couldn't answer your call or respond to your text. I learn from your messages that you have the forensics on the skeleton recovered from Manas's house. Is there anything worth knowing?"

"Yes officer, there is. If you come over, I shall explain."

Soon, Abinay and Lance were in the doctor's lab, who looked busy as always. But what they saw him doing was something they hadn't seen him do ever before. The doctor was immersed in moulding a skull with clay. Intrigued, Lance asked, "Are you indeed doing what I think you are doing, doctor?"

Still drowned with all his focus on the skull he was moulding he spoke, "I am only a forensic doctor officer, not a mind reader. I'll not know what you are thinking. Please enlighten me."

Lance was used to Dr Pashupathi's sarcasm and took it in good humor. "Facial reconstruction!"

"I am mighty impressed, officer Lance! You too are learning on your job, inspired by your chief, is it?"

Lance's smile widened and he felt really good that his efforts were being noticed.

"Yes, I am reconstructing the face for the skull your chief brought me as a gift."

"Will you be actually giving a face to the skeleton? That could give this case a whole new direction."

Looking at his junior enjoying the limelight, Abinay let him continue to bask in it. Lance continued at his enthusiastic best, "But you surprised me with your artistic side, doctor."

"You know, this isn't just dry and boring hard science, but a mix of both amazing science and creative art. If the balance doesn't get right, the pendulum can swing way too much to one side and affect the end result. Too much of science and face will end too sterile and unmoving. But the fact remains, no two facial reconstruction experts can give the exact same face.

"Trust me gentlemen, you have nothing to worry. I will reconstruct this person's face with a minimum of 90% accuracy. The progress the facial re-constructors and forensics across the globe have made today is immeasurable. Scientists have re-constructed faces of people who have been dead for thousands of years and the results have been astonishing.

"But before I tell you what will be done to reconstruct the face, let me tell you the details I have been able to find out. To begin with, the victim is male, aged between 63 and 64. Looking at the wear and tear of his joints, it seems he was quite hefty. The crack you see in the real skull is an injury, the cause of his probable death. But I am sure he was tortured, before he finally died."

"How long has the man been dead, doctor?"

Dr Pashupathi exhaled deeply then said, "That is hard to say, officer. The condition of the body or whatever remains it is in, it could take several months to several years to get to it. Academically, the decomposition of a dead body, be it human or any animal has five stages. As you might guess, this particular body is in the fifth and final stage, it's called the dry remains.

"The rate of decomposition of a body depends on several factors, surrounding temperature, whether the body was exposed to air or water and the number of bacteria present. The more the exposure to these factors, the faster the decomposition. Hence it is hard to specify the time since death.

"Now coming to the facial reconstruction, I am not only using this clay model for measurements of facial muscles. Along with it I also have a 3D-printed skull, DNA analysis, dental plaque and radiocarbon dating. We will be able to build an accurate model. Once you have a face identification of the victim, it will be much simpler."

Stepping forward Abinay agreed and nodded in agreement. "Great job, doctor! You carry on; we too have lots to do. Chief, isn't that right?"

Abinay enquired ruffling his junior's ungroomed hair. The two cops were on their way to the cyber department. While Lance was discussing forensics with Dr Pashupathi, Abinay had learnt from the cyber chief that the series of alphabets that were decrypted from the series of digits was indeed the swift code of a Cuban bank.

"What has a Cuban bank got to do with this case now? You will send us on a wild goose chase, you are good for nothing." Lance demanded banging the table in Manish's cabin.

"What do you mean, officer?" Manish roared, stamping his feet.

"Hold your nerve, both of you. Your tempers will not fetch any answers, your patience will. What is wrong with both of you? I know this case has been difficult, but we cannot lose our minds now. This is exactly what that rogue expects, that we get distracted in our ego trips and lose track of him. We cannot afford to do that. Let us focus guys, this is the true test of our character."

Abinay exploded in response to the sudden feud, after a moment of cold stares. The hot heads of both men cooled down; Lance apologized for losing his temper. To which Manish responded with a warm handshake. In a few minutes, sanity had returned to both of them.

"As I told you, officers, I ran checks on the decrypted text that you had shared. It turned out to be a swift code of a Central Bank of Cuba. I too was perturbed when I got to know, then I decided to do a deep-dive to investigate. As I had a hunch that this could lead to an anti-money laundering case and much more.

Because this is a case of external affairs, we'd need approvals from higher authorities to proceed officially."

Lance, again, was about to interrupt. But then Manish interfered, "Don't fret, gentlemen. I know we don't have the time to wait for formalities. Lives are at stake. There is an alternative way that might work, and I have already employed it. Before you probe any further, my contact in the system has a deep asset in Cuba. He knows something really bad about someone really big in that country. He can pull some strings and might be able to extract the information we need. I have already put him on the job. I expect him to respond anytime now."

Just then, Manish's computer beeped, indicating an internet voice call on his secure network. It was from the deep asset in Cuba. Manish signalled telling the men to maintain complete silence and began the conversation. There was no exchange of words, probably Manish was asked only to listen. The conversation went on for long. Abinay waited patiently, but Lance was as curious as a cat. His mind had triggered unbearable curiosity and it needed to be quenched.

"Chief, I understand this was a very important conversation, but the curiosity is killing me. Please help me understand how this was achieved? Who is this deep asset? How did he get involved?"

Abinay patted Lance comfortingly, "Relax, my friend. I shall tell you everything you want to know. The whereabouts of a deep asset are always confidential for the mission's success and their own security. These details won't be shared, but in most cases these deep assets are spies in a different country on some secret mission. These missions could be combative in nature, or only information-seeking. Sometimes petty criminals too work as informers; they offer to use their qualification into the dark world to access and provide critical information in exchange to their freedom."

The two men then waited for Manish to finish the conversation. There was nothing but a curious silence in the room and it was very loud. It grew even more daunting as Manish's muted conversation continued. Finally, when the call got disconnected, the expression on Manish's face was not a pleasant one. He rolled his fingers in his hair and wore an anxious look on his face.

"Guys, this isn't just a murder case, it's much bigger than we can think of. The things that the deep asset revealed to me are mind boggling.

Both Abinay and Lance were listening to Manish without even blinking. The cyber-crime chief continued, "The deep asset pulled some strings and forced the bank to track the details of the account that we needed. After which he learnt that this account had appeared in the list of the accounts whose transactions seemed shady more than a few times in the bank's internal audit.

"Obviously, because of multiple reasons like the amount being small, the auditor's negligence or even because the country isn't equipped with strong anti-money laundering policies, the slippage might have occurred.

"Furthermore, when the bank's internal audit team probed deeper, they found that the inflow of money to this account came from various countries. None of these accounts had any credibility. When our deep asset back-tracked the money trail, he learnt that all the money had gone through a money-laundering cycle. It is clear that all of the money was generated from dirty sources. The worst part is that the beginning of the entire money trail was found to be crypto currency.

"Finally, the deep asset gave me the name of the account holder – Bali. He also said he would share a picture that was recovered from the bank authorities. We might receive it any time now."

A couple of seconds later, a middle-aged man's image was received.

"He is your man boys. You run a search for him in your criminal records and proceed in your investigation. He, if captured, would be a major witness."

Lance immediately circulated the image across police stations with a 'Wanted' alert on it. But Abinay noticed Lance's crossed eyebrows. He was not satisfied with Manish had told them.

"What is it that is troubling you, Lance?"

"Chief, what is going on? What is this new demon crypto currency? Above all, why are we leading our investigation all the way to Cuba?"

"Hold your horses, Lance, go easy on yourself. We will answer all your questions. Cryptocurrency is virtual currency, it is an innovation in the world of finance. It was created in the wake of the 2008 financial crisis that had rocked every country economically, that too very badly. People had lost trust in every financial institution, including banks, globally. Because they wouldn't be entirely in control of their own hard-earned money.

"Moreover, the anxiety escalated because common people could end up getting their financial assets seized by these institutions, even governments. The ones who created crypto-assets believed the power of a person's money must lie completely in effect with the one who earned it. Not with any bank who keeps it or the government with the power to seize it.

"The rationale behind the innovation was to engage people in financial transactions, without relying on banks or governments. It is a peer to peer transaction, no one controls anybody's money, except themselves. It gives freedom to do what you want with your money at any time, with anyone and anywhere in the world.

"The striking feature of cryptocurrency is that it isn't issued by any centralized bank, hence making it immune to any federal or government interference and manipulation. This gives crypto-assets and transactions an element of anonymity, much like black money dealings. Thus, the introduction of cryptocurrency has revolutionized the money laundering industry."

Abinay rose to his feet and began walking out of the cabin, only to being interrupted by his subordinate. He mimicked the response of the *Terminator*.

"I'll be back!"

After a quick break, the trio was back in the cabin with their cups of hot steaming coffees, but Lance kept his on the desk while the other two sipped theirs. "Drink up boy, you have had a long day so far,"

"But chief..."

Abinay raised a toast with his coffee mug, insisting Lance to sip his coffee and resumed talking.

"Have you heard of FATF? Financial Action Task Force is an inter-governmental organization set up to combat money laundering. One of their tasks is to classify countries into black, grey and white lists. It is obvious to say that black-listed countries are the ones with the weakest anti-money laundering policies. The grey listed countries are the ones which are showing an improving trend. The white list, needless to say, are those countries with the strongest anti-money laundering policies.

"Cuba, not so long ago, was one of the black listed nations by FATF. Though recently it has been enlisted in the grey list, there is a lot that needs to be done in terms of policy making to combat money laundering. Hence it makes Cuba a very intelligent choice to carry out any illegal operations."

Nodding his head sharply and moving his hands frantically, Lance continued to probe, "Point taken chief, I agree that weak anti-money laundering laws make Cuba a potential hub of illegal operations. I also agree that characteristics of cryptocurrencies make it a very suitable option of payment for illicit activities globally. But that does not mean that crypto-assets cannot be used for legal operations. This man in the picture might be in a clean business with his cryptocurrencies. He might be innocent."

"Yes, that is very much possible, but that doesn't negate the possibility of his being involved in crime. Moreover, he is the only link that connects Yuyutsu and Manas. We have to interrogate him at least. If he is found innocent, we let him go. Not only that, we might be saving his life from grave danger. With a killer at lose, he might as well be the next target."

Abinay hopped on to his feet and this time around he winked at Manish saying, "Adios amigo!"

Probably Abinay was in a happy mood, maybe he felt he had got a major breakthrough and was close to nabbing the killer.

"Alright gentlemen, it's been a long day. Let's catch up on some rest, we have loads to do tomorrow. Lance, you've got two people to find, this man in the picture and the dead man whose face Dr Pashupathi would reconstruct by tomorrow. I want every bit of information there is under the sun available about both."

▼

The next morning, while Abinay was driving to the headquarters, his phone beeped with a WhatsApp message. He parked the car to take a look as he was expecting Dr Pashupathi to share the re-constructed face of the dead man. It was an image shared by the forensic expert. Abinay punched the air in excitement and forwarded the image to Lance, asking him to run a search of missing persons' report on the image.

Just then a call from an unexpected number disrupted his thoughts. The call was from Anvesha Roy, the historian. He was intrigued by the call, as he wasn't expecting it. But then he didn't delay picking the call because he suspected the killer to watch or even target her as she had provided information on the case. It didn't matter whether the information was useful or not.

"ACP Abinay! Please help me, I need your help."

"What is it, ma'am? Why do you sound so anxious? Are you safe?"

"I am safe, ACP Abinay, but I am not sure if my brother is. I have been trying to reach him...." She broke into tears as she spoke and it was followed by uncontrollable sobs.

"Don't fret ma'am, I am close to your residence. Please send the exact location. I'll be there as soon as I can. Please do not open the door for anyone till I reach."

Abinay drove as fast as he could and reached the location. He knocked on Anvesha's door. She opened the door literally scared to the core. As she saw him, she sighed in relief and invited him into the house.

"I am grateful you came, officer!"

"That is my duty, ma'am. I am expected to serve civilians. You need not thank me. Now tell me what is bothering you so much about your brother?"

Anvesha inhaled deeply, wiped the sweat beads shining like pearls on her forehead and spoke in a broken voice, "It's been three days since I am trying to reach out to my brother, Vikrant. But he hasn't responded to any of my calls or messages. Till last night, I waited with a hope that he would respond, because he always did after he got over his mood swings. That would usually last for a day or two, but not this time. I wanted to caution him to be careful, as you had warned me that I could be watched. As I thought he being, my kin, could be in trouble."

"Do you guys live together? And what are these mood swings you are talking about? Does he have any depression or any other temperamental issues?"

Anvesha sunk into the sofa, depressed and hiding her face behind her palms.

"The last time I forced him to get examined by this doctor, he was diagnosed schizophrenic. This was two years ago, but he was found to be hyperlexic since he was six. Hyperlexic, meaning…"

Abinay interrupted, "Which type?"

"He was diagnosed as II and III border line back then."

"Then he must have a very high IQ."

"Yes, books have been his only friends, he has never had any friends, he could learn about any subject very quickly. Vikrant had mastered the entire *Bhagavad Gita* at the age of eight and all the Vedas by the time he reached adolescence. But he had no social life, and this condition worsened after my father went missing. He loved our father dearly, he was his role model, extremely passionate about whatever he did or thought.

"Vikrant had done his honours in history after journalism and wanted to become an investigative journalist like my father. Unraveling the truth was his greatest passion."

"When did you discover symptoms of schizophrenia in him?"

"I'll always be guilty and will regret not paying any attention to him or my father. Father used to say that Viki imagined things and talked to himself. I only realized his condition when I saw him talk to himself, hallucinating, as if he was talking to our father, months after father had gone missing."

"Can I see his picture? I'd need it to share it across police stations, your father's too if you have any.

Anvesha wasted no time in sharing both the pictures from her mobile phone. He saw Vikrant's photo, but as soon as he saw her father's picture, his forehead curled into worried lines. He had just realized that the re-constructed face of the skeleton Dr Pashupathi had shared and the one shared by Anvesha as her father resembled a lot. It troubled him that he had to be the messenger to bring the grave news.

Abinay was about to utter the news but was interrupted by a crunchy noise at the window behind him. In a blink of an eye an arrow had fizzed past him and gotten stuck on the wall in front of him. Anvesha burst into a scary scream.

They rushed to the window side to see if they could find anything, but they could see nothing. Then Abinay went to the arrow. As expected, it was tagged with a note.

Do not share your secrets, otherwise they will destroy you.

Abinay was stunned to learn that the killer was following him, but he felt it was better not to show his surprise to the lady.

"Can you relate to this note, Anvesha?"

She shook her head indicating she didn't, but her sub-conscious lingered to something she couldn't pin point to. Both of them pondered on what was the note indicating to? For a moment, Abinay was habitually forced to doubt Anvesha. But his experience and judgment did not allow him to sit on that doubt.

A moment later, both muttered together, "Chanakya!"

"This is Chanakya's quote." Abinay pointed out earnestly,

Anvesha fell silent for a second, as if she was recalling something.

"Vikrant was literally obsessed with Chanakya. It was his obsession that drew me towards learning and researching about the secret society of the Mauryan period. He read and re-read the *Arthashastra* of Chanakya, god knows how many times. It is a widely accepted fact officer that the book is one of the finest political and war discourses ever written in prose.

"But Vikrant would say he found something new each time he read the book. Such was his obsession. He believed if our country is governed as prescribed in the book, we could be doing much better for ourselves and the world. There are not many conversations I can remember with him, but this one about *Arthashastra* is unforgettable. More so, because it convinced me that I must research about what Chanakya and all his principles were all about.

"Vikrant always said that among the fifteen chapters of *Arthashastra* that spoke of different aspects of governance, espionage was his favourite chapter. He was irresistibly fixated on Chanakya. According to him, the espionage system was the backbone of the great governance of the Mauryan empire. The organization of the secret service was uninhibited and was recommended for a variety of purposes, including keeping a vigil on the administration, keeping the conduct of officials corruption free and much more.

"Spies were chosen from various disciplines. There were students, ascetics, farmers, businessmen, religious leaders, news agents. Probably it was the book that inspired him to become an investigative journalist like my father."

"But Anvesha, didn't it occur to him that if the espionage system in the Mauryan Empire was so evolved and strong, it has to be state sponsored?"

"It did, but his argument in defense was that the intention of the state or king in this case was the larger good of the masses and not the selfish intent of being in power. There is indeed no doubt that the Mauryan Empire was infact the golden period in Indian history. The core message of *Arthashastra* is to make any king or head of state understand that any personal motive or benefit cannot be bigger than the good of the nation and its citizens."

"Any idea what he was talking about when you saw him talking to himself, as if to your father?"

"He was mentioning some secret details that father had left for him and were related to father going missing. When I asked him about it, he avoided me, and the same night, he was gone. But around six months ago when I accidentally saw him, I followed him to his house. Somehow, I convinced him to at least keep in touch through calls, if he did not want to return and stay with me."

Abinay then took a moment and spoke in a somber voice, "I did not know when I arrived here that I will have to be the bearer of the bad news to you. But I regret to tell you that we have found your father's skeleton."

Anvesha freaked out and held his collar, "What are you saying, officer? How can you be sure that a random skeleton is my father's?"

Abinay took a deep breath to calm his nerves down and then spoke, "I am not just blabbering anything that comes to my mind. A qualified forensic expert conducted due scientific procedures and re-constructed the skeleton's face. I had no idea who the face belonged to until you shared your father's picture. It brings me immense grief to tell you that your father is indeed dead. But I also promise I shall do everything in my capacity to bring your brother safely back to you."

Anvesha's eyes trickled tears but then she spoke in a very feeble voice, "I know officer, I just don't want to accept this harsh truth. Me and my brother both feared this day for a long time. More so since the police started to ignore our pleas to find our father. I gave up, but Vikrant did not. He still keeps trying to find my father's whereabouts."

Abinay consoled Anvesha, took the address of the place she had followed Vikrant to six months ago and her brother's phone number. He left after cautioning her to be careful and collecting the arrow stuck in the wall. As he drove, Abinay called Lance.

"Chief, I ran searches on both the shady businessman and the dead victim whose skeleton we found. No missing report has been filed for the dead man, but I found the whereabouts of the businessman. He has no criminal record in the past. Apparently, he started as a small-time businessman who had a small pharmacy in the beginning, but gradually expanded his business. I have found his address, he lives alone and I am headed there.

"I tried calling him, but the number is switched off. I found out that he is flying back from Mumbai. His flight will be landing in an hour."

"That isn't good Lance, his life is at risk. He could be killed on the flight. Do one thing, reach the airport and escort him to our station. Make sure you travel with him, take a paramedic and some sharp officers with you. We need to be well prepared, this could turn really ugly. You need to be very vigilant. I want you to bring him safely into custody."

Lance was very curious to know what was going on. He learnt all that had unfolded at Anvesha's place from his chief and how he suspected Vikrant to be the killer of all three – Yuyutsu, Manas and his cook. Of course, the cook's death could be collateral damage.

Abinay parked his jeep a little far from the apartment he had to enter. He didn't want to be spotted. He took his gun, confirmed that it was loaded, fit a silencer to it and set out towards Vikrant's flat. He was in civil dress and so no civilians thought of him as a cop investigating a triple murder case. All the flats on the floor he walked into were locked. The place looked deserted. May be because residents had gone to work.

The flat that Anvesha had mentioned as Vikrant's was a small one. Abinay pulled out his gun and shot at the locked door to barge into the house, pointing the gun forward. There was no one in the house, and it was dimly lit as all the windows were closed and curtains drawn. He switched on the light to increase visibility. The drawing room was haphazardly organized. But he didn't find anything suspicious.

At the corner of the drawing room was another closed door on which was stuck a note with another quote of Chanakya. *Repay your debt till the last penny, eliminate your enemy without any trace.*

He barged into the room and found it spick and span. Totally unlike the drawing room, it was full of things of his interest. There was a white board on the wall on which were names and pictures of Yuyutsu, Manas and the businessman with their names and daily routines. Yuyutsu and Manas's photos were crossed, probably it meant they were successfully eliminated. Bali's picture was clean, which meant he was in line for elimination. Alongside these pictures was a blank page on which was a cross mark. Abinay read it as X, wondering if that was to denote someone unknown.

Abinay rang Lance's number to know Bali's status.

"Chief, I have Bali by my side. I have gotten him medically examined. He seems to be in good health. I am bringing him to our station. He is my responsibility."

Abinay then continued his investigation at Vikrant's house. He found proofs of their financial transactions and USB drives. He collected all the evidence he could lay his hands on and left for the headquarters. Shortly, he along with Lance were interrogating Bali in a police cell.

▼

"Listen Bali, I am no mood to be dramatic. I give you a choice; you quickly blabber out all the secrets you are holding in your chest. Or I put one bullet from up-close right in your head in the next couple of minutes. The choice is completely yours. I can do one favour to you. I can grant you two minutes to make your decision."

Abinay set the stop watch application to two minutes in his mobile and checked the magazine of his gun. It was loaded. Abinay's behaviour ran chills through Lance's spine too, let alone Bali. Even Lance hadn't seen such a dark face of Abinay till date. The stop watch ran out of the set two minutes and Abinay was with his gun and a silencer fitted on it.

Without waiting for the next second to pass, Abinay pressed the trigger of his gun. A bullet passed millimeters next to Bali's right ear and got stuck into the wall behind him.

Bali fell to Abinay's feet, "Officer, I beg you, please don't kill me! I will tell you everything you want to know. I have committed no crime. I was only doing my business till one day I was sent a bag full of money and asked to go to Cuba and set up a pharma company and a research lab there in my name. I know nothing more sir. I get my cut of money every month. I have no idea what goes on in that lab. I had orders to allow these scientists who got killed recently to use my Cuba account."

"I have only heard rumours that they used my lab to work on some secret projects. The end result of which would cause mass destruction and cause irreversible damage. I can only imagine that the money I used to get was a part of some dirty business. But I was too greedy to think all that. Please do not kill me, officer, please. Please!"

"What is his name? What did he look like?"

"He calls himself Mr X and he only calls from an internet phone, there is no other contact. I have never seen him."

Abinay was too furious to talk. He slapped Bali so hard, it made his ear bleed. He walked out of the cell, asking Lance to record the confession. By the time Abinay reached his cabin, he had regained reasonable amount of his composure. He sat on his chair and sipped a bit of water. His hands were tossing the paperweight from one hand to another and his mind was tossing onc option after the other on what best he could do to get his hands on Vikrant.

Suddenly, he recalled the USB drives recovered from Vikrant's hideout. He plugged it in and copied the contents. He was about to play its content, when his mobile beeped. It was a WhatsApp message. Abinay opened it to take a look, as it was his department phone. The received message was a video message from an unknown number. He played the video.

A man in the video was showing his back to the camera, probably he was using a tripod to hold the mobile. He was wearing the same jacket Abinay had been trying to track. Slowly he turned around and unmasked himself.

"By now you know me officer. Yes it's me, Vikrant. I am the man you have been chasing."

He broke out in a sinister laughter, without an iota of regret in his voice or face for what he had done. In fact, Abinay saw pride. The video continued...

"I wanted to congratulate you on the job you have done. If not for you, no one could have saved that greedy monster in your custody now."

The man in the video suddenly slapped himself so hard that the corner of his lower lip started bleeding. He sweat profusely and rage in his eyes wasn't sane. He continued, *"I have to punish myself on failing to give him the punishment he deserves. I wanted to congratulate you and your system for the time being on saving him. But do not think for a moment that I committed these murders only to avenge my father's death.*

"No officer, it wasn't just a personal motive. By now you might have figured out that Yuyutsu and Manas were involved in a lot of dirty business. My father found all about their destructive intent and wanted to expose not only them, but the master mind behind the plan. My father tried everything in his capacity to expose these beasts. It is needless to say that your filthy corrupt system not only ignored him, but also helped them to eliminate the honest man.

"These scientists I killed may be geniuses, but they had no intent of using their intellect for the betterment of humanity. Instead, in the wake of greed and ambition, they were working towards destruction at large. They weren't just my enemies, but the enemies of humanity. My mission was to eliminate these foes with no trace left.

"My father had probably figured out that he will be captured sooner or later. Hence had not just protected the evidences he collected, but also made necessary arrangements to punish the guilty through me. I am ashamed, I couldn't finish the job. It was the guilt of the innocent cook's death that didn't allow me to attack Bali openly. I couldn't risk innocent lives. It was my inability that I couldn't get him before you.

"I know, my father wouldn't have agreed with my approach. People like you and my father still believe in the system. But there are enough examples of loop holes in the system that let the guilty get away with all their wrong doings. But not for long. I am sure